Walki

Mercier Press, 82c Ballyhooly Road,
St. Luke's, Cork, Ireland

Published by Mercier Press, 2025
Copyright © Mary O'Donnell, 2025

The moral rights of Mary O'Donnell to be identified as
the author of this work have been asserted in accordance with
the Copyright and Related Rights Act, 2000.

All rights reserved. This book is copyright material and must not be copied, reproduced, transferred, distributed, leased, licensed or publicly performed or used in any way except as specifically permitted in writing by the publisher, as allowed under the terms and conditions under which it was purchased or as strictly permitted by applicable copyright law. Any unauthorised distribution or use of this text may be a direct infringement of the author's and publisher's rights, and those responsible may be liable in law accordingly.

ISBN: 9781917453226
eISBN: 9781917453400
Audio ISBN: 9781917453417

www.mercierpress.ie

WALKING GHOSTS

MARY O'DONNELL

MERCIER PRESS

Dedicated to readers of short stories everywhere

Contents

1	Cocoa L'Orange	9
2	Stories about Fat People	25
3	Luck	41
4	The Capital of Outer Mongolia	53
5	Like Queens not Criminals	71
6	Peach Jam	80
7	The Space between Louis and Me	93
8	The Stolen Man	107
9	The Creators	120
10	Edna	139
11	All We Can Do Is—	154
12	I'm So Lucky	173
13	Lifting Skin	186

14	Wheelchair Plaza	198
15	Coins for the Ferryman	216
16	Walking Ghosts	226
17	Peace, Love & Pushpanna	240
	Ackowledgements	251

I

Cocoa L'Orange

Like a crouching battalion, the thirty houses in Heatherbell Way nestle along the incline of the mountain. The McEntee's long landing window is positioned directly opposite the window of the Kearney's master bedroom, slightly to the left of its en suite bathroom.

Since the first lockdown, Jake Kearney has spent more time than usual in both bedroom and en suite, attending to bodily grooming, or sometimes, slumped on the side of the bed, doing a quick scan of the novels left around by his wife Sasha. She considers reading to be a positive thing. Jake has never bothered with fiction, preferring non-fiction and biographies.

His reading is urgent, he knows that. His eye leaps paragraphs ahead over hundreds of words in search of the right one, the meaningful one that will explain everything for him, even when he's not quite sure what the question is in the first place. At the very least, reading adds another segment to the vast, black-hole hours which must be plugged.

Sasha has full working days. She is needed by others to do a specific task, and might wear tracksuit bottoms while presenting a blouse and sharply tailored navy jacket to the oblong face of the Circuit Court judge. Jake, on the other hand, is aimless. He acknowledges this each time he glances out the bedroom window having just trimmed his toenails and treated the mottled patches of his toenail fungus yet again, to find himself staring into the face of his neighbour Ned, whose doleful dark eyes and cockroach brows appear, apparition-like, every few days. Ned reminds him of Father Stone from *Father Ted*, the most boring priest on the planet, except Ned isn't a priest, but a locked-down once fashionable greengrocer whose city-centre vegetable and fruit emporium—The Sweet Pea, just off Grafton Street—is closed because everyone is working from home and vegan tourists are a distant memory.

Sometimes Jake nods fractionally at Ned, uncertain as to whether the other man is actually seeing him. He thinks of those suspected propped-up corpses the Russian administration was supposed to have used in the days when a powerful President—ancient and ill—could not be seen to have actually died but wasn't so alive either. Sometimes Ned nods back. They stare into one another's faces. Then Ned usually turns away and withdraws into the gloom of his landing.

Before lockdown, they rarely did more than glance and wave from car to car. Ned drove an upgraded vintage Rolls Royce that sailed forth magisterially whenever he sat into it; it's in the garage now, unused. Jake's Prius Hybrid has cooled its environmental jets as there's no place to go and nobody to visit. His business has also folded. Sofia, his Estonian co-worker and the best chocolate-maker he's ever employed, has moved on in search of a means of surviving.

He misses work in the small factory outside Bray. He also misses Sofia because she was a good laugh and an antidote to Sasha's serious ways, as well as being a reliable worker. She knew how to use the enrober, the truffle-rolling machine and the coating machine. Her chocolate was perfect, heated and mixed just the right amount to form crystals. He could pop out for the occasional half hour for bank business or to check in with one of the other small business owners in the industrial park, knowing she knew what to do.

He doesn't understand the fuss about people putting on weight during the first lockdown and then later on in the second one. Whatever those tubbies are shovelling into themselves it isn't his artisan chocolate, which is gathering mould in the unheated factory where the sun sometimes streams in and turns the air to a broiling stew. He managed to get rid of what was hygienically safe to sell, then resorted to selling bags of broken chocolate to the local kids, who turned up on the doorstep, keen as ferrets once the word got out.

Thursday is Sasha's self-care day. He can hear the soft but clear voice of her yoga master coming through on Zoom in the next bedroom. 'Breathe in . . . now hold for 5 . . . and breathe out again, remembering to hold in those abdominals . . .'

Sasha is relentlessly maintaining herself, determined to follow the rules and survive. Despite her evening breakouts with the wine she hasn't gained an inch of flab due to bi-weekly sessions with a body-coach. That she has a job while he hasn't is something that registers as an ongoing siege by his own jealousy. He never says anything embittered but it leaks out anyway, with a sudden need to pace up and down the hall when she's chortling easily with a fellow professional on the laptop screen.

Unlike him, she's always had tribes of friends. She's part of a cosy little bubble of five, and when they're not having their TGIF glass of wine, they're meeting at a safely maintained distance of two or more metres outside a café. There's Sasha, Sebastian, Fionn, Cathy and Wynette. *The Famous Five*, he tells himself cynically. All they need is the dog Timmy and they'd make a complete Enid Blyton of it.

He checks his watch. She'll be finished in half an hour, he reckons, by which time it will be his turn to have some kind of dinner underway. He ponders the question of what they might eat and makes his way downstairs. There'll be time enough tomorrow to stare back at Ned. He reckons they've found a rhythm, and admits to some slight release in staring at another man in the same boat as himself.

It's all in a look. Each stares into the face of the other; observes, watches, traces the blank misery, the despair, the tamped down maleness of the other. At least, he hopes Ned feels the same. The truth is, the virus might as well have caught them both by the balls and twisted hard.

He opens the fridge and scans the shelves. Smoked salmon no, eggs no. He pulls out the meat drawer to find the usual unused packs of bacon and sausages. He wonders why they both avoid having a damn good fry-up, as if bacon and sausages alone raised cholesterol. In his case the cholesterol lay in 'the widow maker', the cardiac man at the south city clinic informed him. Maybe twenty percent build-up in that left anterior descending artery, or the LAD, he joked. Jake's hunch is that Sasha's is elevated because of the wine she consumes. What is it now, half a bottle a night? When he raised the matter with her, she became defensive and told him he was trying to control her. He sighs as he contemplates an aubergine and two red peppers.

He continues to peer into the fridge, regarding a stack of cholesterol-lowering dairy drinks. Then, unbidden, an image of his finest chocolates floats to the surface of his mind, crushing him. Glossy, buttery, *Tír na nÓg* mouthfuls of ecstasy. Straight from the Land of Youth in the old legend in which Oisín and Niamh of the Golden Hair rode on a mighty white horse. He used to call Sasha his Niamh of the Golden Hair, when her hair was long and fair. Tears begin to prickle in his eyes as he recalls the weekly cargo flown fresh to New York, Boston, Chicago and LA.

Completely steamed up now, he slams the fridge door shut and rummages in the freezer. Finds two pieces of sea bass, solidly frozen. Picking up pace—it's 5.30 and Sasha will appear soon—he finds a platter, shoves them in the microwave to thaw, then grabs the single aubergine and the two peppers before gathering potatoes from a bucket near the sink. Garlic, he thinks, where's the fucking garlic? A single clove lurks at the bottom of the vegetable basket. He unpeels it and starts to chop fiercely, forehead perspiring.

'Thanks, I'm starving.' Later, Sasha glides into her place at the table in calm post-yoga demeanour. Having prepared and cooked the meal, he feels slightly calmer.

'Yum, amazing!' she murmurs, spearing a fragrant red pepper piece on the end of her fork and slipping it hungrily between her lips. Mollified, he smiles.

He'd consulted *Rick Stein's Secret France* for the recipe. The aubergines were sliced and salted for half an hour before he fried them in virgin olive oil with the peppers, after which he added a tin of crushed tomatoes and the miserable squidge of garlic clove. Then sea bass, fried gently, and seasoned boiled potatoes garnished with a dash of horseradish. He considered it a tasty basic meal.

'I'm out tomorrow with the gang,' Sasha remarks.

'Walking. Again?'

'Yes. Why?'

He murmurs quickly, 'I just wondered. Didn't mean anything.'

'Menlo Forest is open, thank Christ.'

'Coffee afterwards in that café?'

'Outside it.'

'What if it rains?'

'I've checked the weather app. Grey but dry tomorrow.'

He senses she's as fed up with him as he is with her after months of fairly civilised getting along, collaborating on this and that domestic project, though in truth collaboration meant capitulation to Sasha's ideas on everything domestic, not that he'd say as much. On impulse, he reaches across and catches her gently by the wrist. She looks up, surprised.

'What?'

Even the snappy sound of the 't', the half-annoyed frown on her brow, irritates him but he persists. 'I just wanted to hold your hand, that's all.' There were no words to cover the terrain of wobbling emotions and future uncertainties. Those available to them might, he suspects, be vicious.

She relinquishes her arm and eases her palm against his. 'I guess we don't do enough of this.'

'You know we don't.'

She squeezes his hand lightly, forking a piece of fish towards her mouth with her free hand.

He observes her chewing, brows slightly dipped as if concentrating either on the eating or on thoughts of what's happening between them.

'The truth is . . . I suppose . . .'

He knows what's coming.

'. . . I do get a bit exasperated with you.'

He waits.

'You're a good man, a great man in fact, but you drive me fucking mad, right?'

He's amazed at how casually patronising she can sound. 'You grind my gears too,' his reply emerges, a calm statement.

Her eyebrows perk up. He nods again. 'That's the truth.' He holds her stare.

'What the hell have I done?' She snaps her hand back from his.

'Nothing specific. I mean, neither of us has *done* anything—'

He falls silent as a new wave of despair washes through him, and her face freezes over to contain the emotion which is surely agitating her. It's a face known to him for more than twenty-five years, one which has radiated the kindest of signals and signs, the most ecstatic too, when on holiday and they were free, a face cool and dispassionate in the courts, but which could break with hilarity during the casual suppers they used to throw. This face was his unwritten language, but somehow he can no longer quite translate it. He puts down his fork, swallows quickly. His throat has seized up as if he's about to cry. Again? The virus. That bloody virus, that microscopic ball with the little cartoon feet, that invisible bauble has ruined everything.

'Well,' she rationalises, 'you've lost a business and it has affected you more than you'll admit.'

Now a gear change, soaring ahead beyond fourth, to fifth, into overdrive.

'Eh, I didn't "lose" the business. It's not something I, like, actually tossed away—' he counters.

'Fuck's sake Jake, you're so literal! That's not what I meant—'

'Ned next door is in the same boat, I'm not the only one—'

'What the hell did he expect? A fucking greengrocer's was always going to take the hit, just like a chocolate shop!'

He draws a breath inwards, then exhales gradually. 'It was an *enterprise*, a chocolate *enterprise*.'

'Oh big fucking deal. I'm telling the truth if you'd only listen.'

'I never stop listening. I want to make you happy.'

'Actually, this isn't about my happiness, Jake. It's more about yours.'

'Happiness? My happiness, is that it?' His shoulders shake as he laughs bitterly. 'I never think about happiness these days, you know.'

'We could have it worse,' she adds. 'At least one of us can work.'

'Yes,' he admits.

But she goes on, as Sasha always does.

'If it weren't for me we wouldn't have a roof over our heads, you realise that?'

Now she's done it. Now he feels like swearing. Using the c-word, which she absolutely detests. On it goes for a while, the snapping and snarling like two enraged curs. Opposite them, the television is on mute as the world plays out its filmed day. The eager expressive face of the news reporter in Washington reporting on the despot's latest response to the 'China virus'. Then the home stories. Teacher unions, doctors, frontline workers. A vox pop of cantankerous people blaming overseas Christmas visitors who partied and spread the new variant. The calm but concerned faces of the men in charge asking people to stay at home.

By the time the bickering ceases, they are both following the television even though it's on mute. Sasha has drained her second glass of wine. Jake sips water, more to relax his throat and prevent him from screaming than from actual thirst. He's just told her that if she's finding it all too much she should draw up the divorce papers.

'Feel free!' he shouts, without really meaning it. 'Anytime! We can head off into the blue with all the other silver splitters!'

Sasha ignores this, her expression inscrutable, the way it is when she's in court. They sit sullenly until she shoves an opened pack of bitter orange *Tír na nÓg* in his direction. He accepts, breaks off two squares and slips them into his mouth. The chocolate melts slowly along the inside of his cheeks, all around his tongue.

There will be no divorce. Neither wants it. Sasha clears up after the meal and Jake stretches out on the sofa, tries to concentrate on a book about corvids which she gifted him at Christmas.

The night darkens, deepens. The entire road is silent, each house locked in a thin fog. Somewhere a dog barks, then stops. A front door slams shut. Jake and Sasha decide to sleep separately, mainly because of her snoring. They both blame it on eating late. He blames it on the wine but doesn't say so. Sasha tells him that tomorrow on the forest walk, Wynette and Fionn will bring coffee and rolls, then they'll sing together beneath the high conifers near the lake, and Cathy will certainly embrace a few tree trunks. 'Mad, isn't it,' she whispers in a conciliatory way before he heads into the spare room, 'but whatever takes us through, right?' He nods in agreement, pecks her on the cheek. How good she smells, he thinks, automatically drawing her closer, waiting until she raises her arms to embrace him too. They stand like that outside the spare room, rocking one another. Her head relaxes and she lets it rest against his shoulder. They say good-night, slowly, without kissing. This is enough, he thinks, not quite ready to touch his lips to hers.

Once in the bedroom, he strips to his underwear and throws himself beneath the duvet, then stares at the ceiling for a long time. The pressure of the day subsides. He can still smell Sasha in his arms, a signature skin odour, her delicate musk.

By mid-morning on Friday she has gone to the forest. A wintry sun shines and he has the house to himself. Still in his underwear, he connects to Spotify, checks out his various collections before settling on *Moods Upbeat and Even*. The Kinks, Genesis, Velvet Underground, Ultravox, Tom Waits. The house pulsates with sound. He's feeling creative and intends to do something with chocolate. As usual, he's not certain what the outcome will be, but chocolate is an art form, although Sasha, predictably, views it solely as a business. He stares into the copper bain-marie on the gas hob and lets three drops of intense orange essence and a hint of chilli fall into the chocolate, which gradually melts, the aroma sweet and comforting, hitting his olfactory receptors. Cocoa l'Orange, he decides, his favourite.

He rummages in a high cupboard and retrieves a set of moulds. Diverse shapes, ranging from butterflies to hearts and flowers. Again, he checks the copper bowl. The chocolate is fully melted, bubbling slowly like the warm muds of Rotorua in New Zealand. He'd like to sit into a pool of either warm mud or chocolate right now, to cover his legs, his bollocks, his chest, all the way up to his neck, and rest there until he was a coated, cleansed, saturated chocolate man. Instead, he goes to the hallway and studies himself in the mirror, bowl in hand. He dips his fingers into the chocolate, rubbing fingers and thumb together as if to get a sense of his medium. Then, a dark brown line down his nose. He looks primitive. He looks like a horse in a Cubist painting. The mix is viscous and does not drip. Now a dense curve darkens the path from temple to temple across his high forehead. Two smears on the outer edges of his eyelids, more like dots really. He continues with chocolate lines moving out from the corners of each eye, as if he were in a Chinese opera, then the long downward curve towards his jawline and along the chin.

Already, the chocolate is firming like a mask. He almost laughs but suppresses it so as not to crack the chocolate, which is smooth, so dense and reddish brown. 'Monarch of all I survey,' he intones between his teeth, 'monarch of all I survey.' Then suddenly, another fit of weeping surges, and he is like the crying clown in a circus, as the chocolate cracks and splinters down onto the wooden floor.

'Get busy, man, get busy!' he urges, gulping, catching his breath, wiping his face of chocolate and tears in the downstairs bathroom. When he has tidied up the hall and removed all traces of chocolate, he returns to the kitchen, gets out the bain-marie again and melts a new mix, adding extra orange essence, but slightly less chilli. Carefully he pours the finished mix into the moulds, wondering briefly if such moulds are a bit too feminine. He might have opted for blunt squares, triangles and rectangles. Too late. The chocolate is cooling. Quickly, he slips it into the top shelf of the fridge and tidies up again. He's done three trays.

An hour later, he has changed into a loose muslin shirt and clean jeans. He enters the en suite. He is carrying one mould of fresh chocolate pieces set onto a golden ceramic plate, usually kept for Christmas. The air is still damp from Sasha's earlier shower, and the odour of a drying towel rises from the radiator. The scent of her shower gel—something slightly Scandinavian and outdoorsy, rosemary or birchwood—permeates the air. He places the plate on the edge of the wide sink, then turns towards the window.

Ned is there, his sad eyes boring across the space between the two houses. Jake takes up position and gazes straight back, focusing on the eyes, which are probably a mere twelve feet away if he were to measure it. What a face, he thinks, drinking it in. A grey face with grey eyes and a strong brow, one he knows yet does not know, whose subtle semiotics are his to untangle and explore.

At first he wonders if the frosty sunshine is creating a glare, if Ned isn't actually seeing him. But then recognition creeps along the other man's face, which for a time remains morose, before it twitches in a minor yet perceptible way. He meets Ned's expression. It's all in the eyes, the skin around them crinkling a little, as if with suppressed laughter.

And when the other man slowly raises his hand in what could be a wave or an attempt at reaching out, Jake raises his too. He stretches back to the plate, turns and elevates it with both arms before the window. The sun strikes the golden surface and a series of prismatic rays dance across the space between the houses. Finally, Ned nods again. Jake sees him swallow. Although the sun threatens to soften the chocolate, they stand, transfixed by light, by the golden rim of the platter, its centre dark eye of Cocoa l'Orange.

2

STORIES ABOUT FAT PEOPLE

The instructor glanced at him and waited, not that Ollie noticed as he searched for some nook in which to collapse his body. He lumbered to the far end of the room where someone eventually made an opening which revealed one remaining very low stool. It felt like school, with all the good students present and he, as ever, late.

'I'm Leonie Lefoy,' the instructor said quickly. 'Welcome to Inkspots.' She scanned a sheet of paper on the desk. 'Oliver, is it?'

'Ollie. Sorry I'm late,' he said. He looked around and noted that he was the only man present.

Leonie was talking about what she called 'the Flow', which to his ears sounded like an oblique reference to female problems. She spoke of the river of imagination, and about getting around the obstacles that 'Block the Flow', especially for women. She pursed her lips and glanced in his direction, as if to say this was something he might be personally responsible for.

'Some writers,' she confided, 'insist there's no autobiography in their work, but as far as I'm concerned, this is a distortion.'

You mean a lie, Ollie corrected mentally. He thought about the bits plotted on unused pages in his son's old copybook, the afterthought he'd torn out and shoved in his inside jacket pocket along with the short typed-up first chapter from a thriller. Someday, his novel might appear in the shops with his picture, glowing yet not quite smiling, wisdom in his grey eyes.

Regarding the other thing, the scrap he'd also brought, he still didn't know why he'd begun to jot down his thoughts on the back page of that copybook. One evening when he was alone, Kayla out at what she called her book club which was really a wine and gossip session, their son at soccer training, he had experienced a restlessness which required him to do something other than watch television. He'd sat down at the kitchen table, aware of sounds; two cats shaping up for a brawl in the garden next door, and the vibration of the sound system from the house across the road.

He wrote five pages. It was set in an ordinary house in a town. Its main characters were grubby, as far from glamour as it was possible to be.

He tried to imagine the reaction from people he knew if they actually read it, which he doubted they ever would. Kayla's family would turn on him. They'd savage him like the mad pigs they were, without a second thought. He imagined it now maliciously, the whole family crowded into The Squealing Pig on a Sunday, drinking themselves blind. Family pride was based on the fact that in all the years of Sundays, not one of them had ever fallen over.

He sometimes diverted Kayla from those sessions by tempting her along to sales in the furniture warehouses on the edge of the town, or even by seducing her into bed after dinner, when their son had gone off to play soccer. But the sales only annoyed her because since he'd been made redundant at the restaurant when it suddenly scaled down and no longer needed him as manager they couldn't afford to do more than look.

'Plunder your lives, ladies!' Leonie urged. 'And Oliver too of course!' She gave a little smirk in his direction. 'Turn trauma to profit!' she added comfortably.

Everybody laughed. Ollie looked around, the word 'trauma' smacking his brain like a hand. He recognised three women from the gym, but most of the others were strangers with quilted jackets and furry scarves draped over the chairs.

One woman was thin—skinny, even, like a heroin addict with bulbous eyes—and another was constructed like Mrs Brezhnev, the wife of a Soviet communist leader he remembered from his childhood. Wide, with several chins and a shelf of a chest you could do a headstand on. He forced his eyes away from her.

Then he spotted Malory Thorndike who lived in Aylmer Park. He'd recently done some weeding and pruning for her neighbour Mrs Haley and frequently saw Malory drive out in a purring cream convertible. 'Retired lady,' Mrs Haley had remarked, 'an accountant of some kind.' She had also added that Malory looked incredibly fresh for a woman her age. 'There's a sweet-talking decorator from Riga, never out of it,' she went on, winking at him.

He turned his mind again to writing. What was there to say that would strike anybody as new or startling, if he began to scribble his way into a story about Kayla?

Disappointed Kayla had a cast-iron but sturdy stomach when she undressed and miraculously still occasionally found some use for him. She had arrived home relatively upright the previous night, brought a Chinese takeaway and a bottle of white wine. Then they watched a film on television which he found funny and interesting. It was called *La Ménage à Trois*, about two gays having to face down two respectable provincial parents who arrive at their very camp apartment in the centre of Paris. Kayla, who hated anything to do with homosexuals, found it disgusting.

'They're rampant, don't you know that!'

'Who?'

'Gays. God's sake Ollie! We read this novel at the book club and what it doesn't tell you about the main characters' antics, these two gay guys,' she paused for breath, 'doesn't leave much to the imagination!'

Still, the night had ended amicably with both happy to have sex, and when that happened he occasionally felt calm again. He could cope which was the best he could hope for.

Sex helped but he didn't always feel right about it. Sometimes when he enjoyed her body he had the unsettling feeling that he was using her even when she wanted it. Wasn't that 'rampant' too, as she put it?

But could he write about such subjects? Lots of authors did, he knew that from listening to interviews on morning radio. Plenty of them. People who led clever, higgledy-piggledy lives in remote old schoolhouses in Wicklow or Connemara, or whimsical English types in Shropshire farm houses or cottages in deepest Cornwall, with amusing journalist or dog-breeding wives; they were able to describe in scintillating detail the minutiae of love and make it either hilariously funny or even sad.

'What if the story is a sad one?' a voice interrupted Leonie.

It was his own, he realised.

'Perhaps every story has an underbelly of sadness,' she eventually replied mysteriously.

'I don't think every story is sad,' Ollie said in a matter-of-fact way. 'Only some stories. But does it matter if it's a sad story? I mean, for a beginner like me.'

There was a weighty silence. Heads swivelled towards Leonie as she formulated a response to what some construed as a challenge. She wore a deep pink boiled-wool v-neck sweater and a purple plaid skirt. It offset her black hair and creamy skin. Silver earrings dangled against her neck.

'It doesn't matter if the story is sad,' she responded, 'but it does matter that you make it interesting.'

There were murmurs of assent about this up and down the long table.

'Remember,' she beamed at Ollie as if letting him into a special secret, 'even if your story is sad, you're quite free to also make it amusing.' She gave an example of the work of an Irish writer whose entire career was built on novels about council estates and poverty. Then she mentioned another writer, a Canadian, who specialised in middle-aged 'angst', as Leonie called it.

For some reason, Ollie was suspicious of that word. Kayla had arrived back from one of her book club sessions using it. Every time she felt out of sorts or simply in a bad mood now, she insisted on describing her angst.

Then he heard Malory's voice. 'It's like the two sides of Greek drama, comedy and tragedy, isn't it?'

This question, which was also a very confident statement, seemed to surprise Leonie who arched her left eyebrow.

'That's so true, you know,' she nodded, eyebrow descending again but now dipping seriously as she scrutinised Malory.

*

Leonie had brought in a short story called 'Fat' written by a famous American writer. It described a fat man who orders a gigantic meal from the waitress in a diner. His fleshy immensity is described. The waitress notices his thick creamy fingers. She gives him time to make up his mind before she takes his order. When he refers to himself he says 'we' and never 'I', as if there were several of him stuffed inside his gargantuan body. In the kitchen the other waitresses belittle him, referring to him as her fat friend, but the woman telling the story is excited. It is as if an erotic god has arrived in her life.

When he read the sentence 'God Rita, but those were fingers' a strange, aroused thrill shot through Ollie's balls. Rita was that kind of waitress, with low expectations about everything. It would be like him, weeding Mrs McCoy's garden then being totally knocked off his perch by an encounter with Mrs. McCoy's trim-hipped Lithuanian cleaner. The waitress was not just encountering the fat man but herself also.

He became aware of unease in the room. Then the skinny woman spoke. 'I don't get it. What's the big deal about this guy?'

'Okay, what *is* the big deal about him?' Leonie redirected the question to the group.

'Well,' a woman with a slab of gelled red hair offered, 'it's a really ordinary situation, isn't it? I mean, she's a waitress.'

That amused Ollie. Despite himself, a grunt escaped him. Leonie's head whipped around and again her left eyebrow arched. Again, he heard his own voice.

'Like, waitresses can't have important feelings?' He looked around, remembering the girls from his own restaurant before the bank had moved in.

Gel-hair threw him a look. 'No-oo, not exactly,' she waved her hands as she tried to articulate it. 'But she's dead ordinary, isn't she? And what's the deal about the fat man?'

Leonie intervened. 'Good question, just what is so special about this fat man?'

Then Malory spoke. 'I think what's special is the sexual chemistry between the two of them,' she said dreamily.

'Thank you for articulating that, Malory.' Leonie was nodding slowly in approval.

'Yeah, but he's fat!' someone whooped.

'And perhaps that's what makes him so interesting?' the tutor threw out without smiling.

A sour voice spoke up. It was the woman Ollie had observed earlier. Mrs Brezhnev's purplish face flashed angrily.

'Personally, Ms Lefoy, I think it's a stupid story,' she said.

Leonie blushed. 'Why?'

'It's just stupid!' Her chair scraped back. 'A lone fat man making a fool of himself in a diner? Gimme a break!' she barked, bending to pick up her bag.

'I'm not laughing,' Ollie announced as a cord of silence tightened around the room.

'No, but you think it's a great read all the same, don't you?' The woman jabbed her finger at him.

He felt reprimanded. If the woman was mortally offended, perhaps it wasn't such a great story after all. But then his thoughts became steely as another consideration struck home. It came from years of enduring and daring. He met the woman's eye, then let the words come slowly, deliberately, before he lost his courage.

'As a matter of fact, I think it's a fucking great read. It's hot and sexy from the very first page.'

'Hot? Sexy?' The woman turned to Leonie. 'I'm sorry Ms Lefoy, but stories about fat people are not funny. Stories about fat people are certainly not hot or sexy, as our colleague here calls it . . .' Her voice began to falter. 'I'm sorry, but I'm leaving.'

Leonie clasped her hands together as if in prayer. 'That's your choice entirely,' she said quietly.

Ollie thought he was hearing things. What kind of psycho-crap was that?

'Yes it is my choice!' the woman snapped, indignation rearing over grievance.

'Don't go!' Ollie called out. 'Don't be a bloody eejit!'

'And you watch your language!' the woman barked up the table at him.

'Ollie? If you don't mind,' Leonie eyeballed him, then turned back to the woman. 'It's a story. It's not meant to . . .' She stopped then, uncertain how to continue.

Ollie sputtered. 'But it *is* meant to! It's meant to cut through all the tripe about everything!'

'Ollie, I must ask you not to . . .'

'But that's the point! That story is meant to throw your life upside down!'

'Yes but . . .' Leonie protested.

'And you're a writer!'

Ollie did not add that it was just the woman's luck that she was built like a mammoth. Just as it was his own luck that he could enjoy the ham-limbed, humming-like-bees magnetism of the fat man. Suddenly he saw himself wrestling with that man, naked on a big floor. The image dissolved and then he imagined himself having such an effect on Kayla. All creamy fingers, belly, heavy thighs and silky bone-hard penis, and he suddenly remembered something about desire, not the night-after-the-pub kind he knew so well, which brought as much relief as a good sneeze.

'I'd like to phone you this evening, if that's okay,' Leonie said to Mrs Brezhnev.

'Please yourself,' the woman shrugged before hauling herself, head high, out the door. When it slammed, one or two exchanged looks. The skinny woman smirked.

'Now we know one way the fat man is important. Just goes to prove how a story can be an emotional catalyst,' Leonie said, her tone ascending as if questioning and accusing at the same time.

'Or maybe some people are just bad readers,' Ollie growled at nobody in particular.

The gel-haired woman sniggered.

'There may be a smidgen of truth in that.' Leonie, grim-faced, was shuffling papers.

'Oh for heaven's sake!' the thin woman turned in Ollie's direction. 'Sure we can all read! I read three novels a week!'

They broke for coffee. The women chittered with excitement. During the fifteen-minute break their voices rose higher and, it seemed to Ollie, more raucously as ice broke and bonds were made.

The instructor regarded him. 'So you liked the story,' she said.

'I did,' he said, at first not meeting her eye as he helped himself to coffee.

'Must be tricky, these classes,' he said finally.

'I'm used to it . . .' The skin around her eyes crinkled, almost hinting at humour. He observed the instructor's face again, re-establishing the divide: Successful Writer versus Aspiring Hopeful.

After the break, she asked if anybody had anything they'd like to read aloud.

Gel-hair interrupted. 'What I need to know,' she drawled, 'is where to send my stories.'

Leonie ignored the question and asked if she'd like to read.

'Not today. I didn't come to read so much as absorb, you know? Like, I want a list, with addresses?'

'The list comes at the end of the course when you've written something new,' Leonie replied. 'Now, who wants to read?' she repeated.

Most people shrank from exposure at the first session, so Ollie put up his hand. He was more nervous than he could ever have imagined. When was the last time anyone had heard his declamatory voice? Firing a late order into the restaurant kitchen? At school?

'I'll read this bit of rubbish.' He waved a few pages and laughed self-deprecatingly.

Leonie directed some more psycho-waffle to the group about their Inner Judge, and how they shouldn't assess their own work harshly in advance, as Ollie had just done.

But Ollie was sorting through the pages, which trembled as he held them. It was like trying to control butterflies, to contain fragile wings within his life and within this moment. Words, he imagined, might die as soon as spoken, but if he did not allow these women with their piddling prejudice and fear—lots of fear!—to see the threads of his life, if he did not allow that, he would never be able to make up anything about Kayla and how love can evaporate to something the far side of indifference.

And why hadn't he left? For the usual miserable reasons. Kayla didn't always do his head in, they still had sex, and anyway they couldn't afford a divorce. The drinking only escalated after he lost his job. They told themselves they'd be able to hold onto the house. His son, even at seventeen, continued to cling to the ideal of the family together: Mammy, Daddy, and Son of Mammy and Daddy.

He took a breath, opened his mouth and began to read:

The house was filthy but the woman never noticed. She'd hardly lifted a finger in years. But years before, he carried her over the threshold and her four months gone. They'd tried to get rid of it by taking the fastest bumpiest rides at the funfair in Bray. Although that was all hilarious and they were feckless anyway, not worrying about anything, it was no good. She was up the duff. She listened to him as he told her that everything would be all right, that she could trust him, he was mad for her and did she believe in soulmates and destiny. Back then they staggered, laughing, down the hall and he almost dropped her on the stairs, and when they had collapsed on the new carpet, the cheapest they could find, they'd started to kiss and bite and kiss again.

His voice gave out. Incredibly, he was afraid he might cry. There was the cord of silence again, which felt different.

'Go on,' Leonie urged, and for the first time he welcomed her studied calmness.

He steadied himself. 'I don't think I can,' he said. Again, a thick silence descended on the room and nobody spoke. One of the women whispered to her companion. Leonie looked from face to face. He could hardly hold his hands still and kept smoothing the pages. He had written and uttered the words, pretending they were part of another person's story.

'What you've read is a great start nevertheless,' Leonie eventually said. 'It's something to go on. Beginnings, hints of background and so on.'

Then Gel-hair spoke. 'You . . . you mean he tried to make her have an abortion at a funfair?'

He snapped then. 'Christ. No. I'm not talking about a fucking abortion.'

'What are you talking about then?' Gel-hair was insistent, her face alert. 'It sounds like you're talking about people who want rid of it. I mean, anyone with an unwanted pregnancy might have tried to bang it out of them, I'm not saying you're not convincing . . .'

He held his hand up, shook his head, exasperated. In a way she was right, although that was not his point. Inexplicably then he heard a thread of something in his head. *Love, love, love . . .* just like the Beatles song. It was plain and simple, the only thing that mattered or might endure.

'It's just not about abortion, or getting rid of it. Getting rid of him', he countered in a whisper, thinking of their son.

For the first time Gel-hair looked discomfited. 'Oh,' she said with a slight frown.

He recalled Kayla and the breeze that caressed his soul as they bumped and banged around in the Sky-train, then the Tunnel of Hell, and how that breeze, having long since changed direction, had never quite died. He steadied himself again before these women who believed they knew everything worth knowing, whether as human biology or destiny.

Sometimes they got it wrong.

3

Luck

Punctually at seven in the evening he opens a canvas bag and spreads out his professional equipment. This consists of ten common cockle shells, one speckled Deer Cowrie, and in the centre of the display, his Queen Conch, which never fails to draw comment.

He sits at the corner of a side street not far from the Hotel Balcón de Europa and the Kronox Café. This serves the dual purpose of being visible to Nerja's surging evening crowds along the Plaza near the hotel, as well as to the passers-by drifting up towards the Town Hall.

The first fifteen minutes or so can be quiet, which allows him to observe the thriving enterprise along the street: Gabonese women plaiting children's hair, a couple rehearsing their tango moves before they dance in front of the Balcón de Europa later on, and a guitarist tuning up outside the wine bar. Most of all, he watches the pick-pockets, whom he identifies by their innocent faces, as they wander up and down the street, across to the Plaza and back again, attaching themselves casually behind this or that tourist.

He'd never intended to learn the tarot. In Dublin in the mid-2000s, he had ingratiated himself into the local cultural scene mainly by helping out on the door at poetry readings and book launches and getting to know the better writers and a few well-connected academics. This approach helped him; being present, obliging, and paying attention to the more approachable writers. Gradually elements of the city's diplomatic circles warmed to him too. He was a welcome addition to several merry dinner parties, including one in the new US ambassador's residence in the Phoenix Park, where he held his own and did not drink too much. He was well-read, urbane, and the ambassador was well disposed to his soft west of Ireland accent. In the end though, he'd had to leave in a hurry and felt himself no longer welcome.

His face is darkly tanned, although a scar on his forehead, acquired two years ago when he resisted a thief in the backstreets of Torremolinos, is an irate crimson. He was lucky not to lose the left eye. His green eyes gleam beneath trimmed brown eyebrows.

He concentrates again on the crowds around him. A woman approaches hesitantly.

'How can I help you, madam?' He looks into her eyes.

She clutches a worn blue shoulder bag, the gilt on its clasp long worn away.

'You look fatigued. Have you travelled far?' All part of a method. Solicitousness goes a long way with some of the women.

'Yes. I arrived two days ago. I'd like a reading.' English, he deduces. From London more than likely. Over the years working the coast from Marbella to Tarifa, he has acquired a working knowledge of accents from Hampshire to Aberdeen. He recognises all Irish accents automatically, and throws out a few stock Gaelic phrases which those tourists always enjoy; *fáilte romhat* and *go raibh maith agat*.

Immediately, he grasps the woman's problem. He knows by her long, nervous neck and flat chest, her skinny clueless fingers which have never touched a man, and the anxiety in her pale eyes, that she is probably a Gold Star Virgin suffering from the global disease, loneliness. The women who hunch before him rarely discuss careers, only matters of the heart. Immediately she selects several Minor Arcana from among the cards, including the Ace of Cups. Her choices are well supported by the Ace of Pentacles, indicating that her finances are in good condition. He knows not to dwell on Pentacles, and instead concentrates on the Ace of Cups, her emotional state.

'All will be well,' he murmurs quietly, not wishing the growing queue to overhear what is, after all, a confidential sitting. 'This card,' he points to a card on which are three golden Cups, 'shows that you have great emotional richness ahead.' A hopeful expression breaks across the woman's face. 'I'd even go so far to say that this person who has disappointed you will get his just desserts.' She looks gratified. He stares into her eyes, which soften. He can tell that nobody listens to her, and as the night is only beginning and the exhaustion of listening has not yet struck, he pities her. Nobody ever looks into her eyes for more than the most functional reasons.

'You, Madam, are on the brink of something special, as demonstrated by this card.' He flicks up one of the Major Arcana, The Lovers. 'It means new beginnings.' He pauses to let the words sink in. Near him in the Café Kronos a brazier has just been lit and the glow has created an aura around his hair. The woman's eyes rest on him, her lips slightly parted. 'Trust yourself. And I implore you to forget all the negative energy which the last man brought into your life.'

It's so basic. The woman thinks little of herself. And will continue to, regardless. Now she sits back, pleased. Convinced too, he thinks. Well, if he can make someone happier perhaps his utterances do come true in the end. When it comes down to it so much is suggestion.

The woman goes away, a smile on her face, having paid him twenty-five euro. He pockets the cash in the large inner pocket of his apricot-coloured coat.

An hour and a half pass without incident. The Plaza is busy. The tango dancers draw admiring crowds, inspiring some of the carefree holidaymakers to try tango for themselves. Another woman sits down before him. Something about her causes his eyes to narrow instinctively, even as he welcomes her. Middle-aged like himself, she is tall and tanned with springy grey hair. She wears a yellow sundress, and a heavy coral necklace nestles in the crease of her breasts. He has to force his eyes away from a consideration of her breasts, gazing instead at the teenage daughter who stands beside her in high-cut denim shorts. It's a humid evening and he begins to feel even warmer. He dares not remove the coat despite the heat for fear of the pickpockets who keep an eye on him.

He hunches his shoulders and spreads the cards. His eyes never leave her face as he studies her. She chooses a card. The Empress.

'A very auspicious card, madam,' he begins, adopting his Middle Eastern voice with its rolling 'r's.

'Oh for heaven's sake, tell me something new!' the woman snaps, then sighs in a bored way. Hers is a well-spoken British accent.

'Sorry?'

'Tell me something worthwhile. If you can,' she challenges. From across the small table, he can smell wine and garlic on her breath.

'Madam, I normally charge twenty-five euro for a reading, but in your case, and to ease your doubts, a mere fifteen euros . . .' The woman rummages in her bag and withdraws a purse.

'Here,' she tosses notes on the table, 'Tell me something you can't possibly know and I'll double it,' she grumbles.

A man carrying a small, tranquillised monkey passes by. 'Madam, in your case I also need to see your left hand.'

She thrusts it in his face and he pretends to scrutinise it. She has a very long life line, he notes.

'Please select any cards.'

She turns them over with another impatient sigh.

He stares at the cards. Justice. The Devil. The Ace of Swords. He swallows again.

'Madam, you have an injustice in your life.'

'So? Doesn't everybody?'

'You were deceived many years ago.'

'Weren't we all? Excuse my language, but don't talk bollox.'

He ignores this and takes a deep breath in to steady his nerves. 'Madam, in your case a promise was made but not kept.'

At this, she seems to relent. He glances at the daughter, who observes the proceedings in between playing a game on her phone, her expression a little amused.

'The man was a scoundrel by any standards. He took advantage of your kindness.'

'That's not unusual. He was a shithead, excuse my language again. Tell me something else.'

He studies her, the fine lines, grey eyes, the straight hairline with a strong plume of darker hair to one side.

'These cards, the Ace of Wands and the Ace of Pentacles, tell me you may be an outdoorsy sort of woman? Gardener perhaps?'

'Outdoorsy? Close enough. But then you've seen my hands.' Her left hand is rough and firm, the fingernails straight-clipped and unpolished.

'Regardless, you work in the outdoors.'

'I'm starting to be impressed. I'm a garden designer.'

She tosses her head in the daughter's direction. 'You know I'm only doing this because she asked me to. All you people are charlatans. You don't fool me, even if you've picked up a few tricks along the way.'

'Madam, we don't have to continue,' he says more coolly, reaching inside his jacket pocket. He'd be relieved to return her cash.

'No. Please continue.' He turns over another card. The Magician. 'You are a much-loved lady, great hurt was caused by your . . .' he hesitates, 'I don't wish to be indiscrete, but . . . a significant relationship within your marriage?'

The woman sits very still, her face giving nothing away.

'You confessed? To your husband perhaps?'

He drip-feeds the information. Gently does it.

'My daughter knows all.'

'Everything?'

'Everything.'

The daughter smirks. His own colour rises. A solid queue of women now snakes patiently around the corner.

'You were deceived by this person. He made promises. The person in question is no longer in your life?'

'He did and he isn't,' the woman snorts.

Finally, softly spoken, the words that clinch it. 'But you loved him?'

He points to the Knight. The woman considers this card for a moment.

'He was no knight in shining armour.'

'He broke your heart?'

At this question, she softens. He tilts his head back, his face now in the shade.

'That's what it felt like! Later, all I remembered was lies and deception.' She glances at the daughter.

At this, he too looks towards the daughter. Her brown curling hair, the lustre of her eyes beneath heavy layers of mascara and overdrawn eyebrows. The heat is almost overwhelming, the air so thick with it he can scarcely breathe. He'll have to get rid of this woman and take a break.

'What is it you wish to know?' he asks more briskly.

'I want to know what happened to him. Because I want to confront the bastard. My therapist says I should.'

'Let me assure you madam that there is no point. You are free, because according to this card, the Hanged Man, he is no longer with us.'

'As in, D-E-A-D?' she gapes.

'Possibly. If I'm not mistaken, the man fled to somewhere southern . . . no, northern . . . Scandinavia, perhaps?'

'Yes! He went to Sweden. Go on,' she urges.

He turns over four cards randomly, studies them through half-closed eyes. 'This configuration doesn't augur well. He may be seriously unwell.'

'Really sick? Good, he deserves that.'

'If anything, he may be dead.' He turns one of the cards towards her. 'See this? The Page can represent someone who is a fool, even mentally unstable. He may have come to a bad end.'

The woman sits back now and grins up at her daughter. 'It's all right, sweetheart. I can relax now for the rest of my life.'

For the first time the girl speaks. 'Told you so, Mummy! If you don't look, you won't find.' And she winks at her mother.

'I did hate him for what he did,' she confides again, 'but I've outlived the fucker.' She opens her purse and tosses more notes on the table without counting them. 'Thank you,' she murmurs, 'you've lifted a great annoyance off my shoulders.'

They walk away into the evening, the woman's arm resting along her daughter's waist. Relieved to be rid of them but still nervous, he decides to put up his 'CLOSED TILL TOMORROW' sign, picks up the shells and cards, then drops them into his bag.

*

At ten o'clock he reaches his apartment. It's in an unfashionable area, but also near the hospital, a free gym and a supermarket. It suits him very well. Rebeka is waiting. She sweeps across the room and hugs him. A steaming pan of doro wat is on the stove. He holds her in his arms, then strokes her pregnant belly. He is exhausted, and although he has stopped sweating, feels unclean.

'I should shower first,' he tells her politely.

'You never shower before you eat,' she whispers.

'Tonight is different. It's very humid out there.' More than that, he wants to wash something away. If he can wash his body down, that will do.

Fifteen minutes later, he throws himself down on the frayed sofa Rebeka has covered with a tangerine-coloured woven rug, then rubs his still-damp face thoughtfully with both hands.

'I've had a very lucky night, apart from the money.' He reaches within his coat and places three hundred euros on the table. She gasps.

'One woman gave a third of this,' he tells her.

'Was she mad?'

'Just desperate,' he replies, 'Now buy yourself something brand new tomorrow. Nothing second-hand. A dress? The one you saw last week in that shop.'

But Rebeka is curious, and ignores this. 'Why did she pay so much?'

'The thing is . . . I told her something she really needed to hear.'

He decides to risk telling her more, about a time when she would have been a ten-year-old in Addis Ababa with no sense of where life would bring her and whose arms would eventually enfold her. He tells of his time in Dublin's Georgian squares where homes were large and hosts welcoming. Of his time with the English diplomat's wife, exploring her garden and then writing about it in a newspaper column. Briefly, she became famous around the country.

Back then his hair was cropped very short, he was beardless and unscarred.

'Everyone thought I was so clever,' he says in a low voice, 'and to tell the truth, I almost believed it myself.'

Rebeka's hands fly to her mouth, and she giggles. 'She didn't recognise you?'

'No.'

'And the daughter?'

'The daughter wasn't born when I left. But her husband found out. I had to leave.' She regards him with a steady look that reminds him that she is no fool. 'Men,' she says without smiling. 'Always running away, always leaving a mess behind them. Like my father did.'

'I know I've made mistakes,' he begins, but she places her hand over his, leads him to the table.

'You have,' she replies, moving to the stove and taking the lid off the saucepan. 'But all that is behind you. I pray to Allah for you every day, because you are a good man. And even the tarot told you something tonight.'

He sits down and beholds the meal Rebeka has prepared, which she ladles into a jade-green bowl. He removes his spectacles and places them on a side plate.

4

THE CAPITAL OF OUTER MONGOLIA

After Sunday dinner, they retired to read. Honora spent half an hour going through *The Telegraph* crossword. She had solved all the other clues but for the one about the capital of Outer Mongolia, humming and hawing her way through the cities of Asia, learned long ago in geography books. Her sister-in-law Rose dozed off in front of the window, faded gold hair bathed in afternoon light. Honora's daughter Kay observed her aunt's fingers, draped over the armchair. *You have your Aunt Rose's spidery fingers! You're as dim as Aunt Rose!* a voice from long ago called out in her head.

Kay watched as her mother turned the pages of a small atlas, sidetracked as she scrutinised a map of the Middle East, one finger hovering over Aswan as she reminisced about the Nile cruise she and Paul had taken many years ago.

'That was so wonderful, you know,' she remarked to Kay. 'The desert sand bothered his lungs. Your poor

Daddy always suffered with his lungs. But he had his inhaler, so he was grand.'

Kay nodded, reluctant to join in any discussion with her mother after the dinner conversation half an hour before. Honora had dragged Paul to every luxury desert resort in the Middle East, despite the fact that he was chronically asthmatic.

'It was the quality of service,' she would insist delightedly, 'you couldn't find better hotels any place on the planet.'

Before dinner, everything had been going quite smoothly. The kitchen door had creaked open and Aunt Rose floated in, shoes polished, in a green wool coat buttoned to the neck.

'I thought you might like a newspaper,' she said to Honora, clearing her throat softly as she laid the newspaper on the table.

Seeing Kay, she stopped suddenly and opened her arms wide in a crucifixion-style greeting. 'You're here! Wonderful! How are you, dear?' she exclaimed, hugging her.

Her embrace was a wisp of a touch, scarcely felt by Kay as her aunt's cheek softly brushed her own.

Honora regarded the display stonily. She stirred a white sauce. Since her husband Paul's death, Sunday dinners consisted of boiled bacon, cabbage and white sauce, with a saucepan of potatoes in the middle of the table.

There was little point, she explained often, in getting a roast, when Paul wasn't there to share it. Nonetheless, Honora always got Kay to open a bottle of red and decant it. Then Honora herself would swish, sample and sup before pronouncing it drinkable.

'Your father would approve,' she said now, replacing her wine glass on the table.

For almost a year after Paul died, Kay and her sister Sorcha appeared on alternate weekends to keep their mother company, who had decided that the presence of one or other daughter at weekends was essential. And although Kay herself had a husband and two sons some three hours away, neither was she exempt from the expectation that she or all of them would travel west.

Honora also stated that Sorcha, being single, could surely have nothing better to do at weekends. When Kay once pointed out that Sorcha worked hard all week and that she too was entitled to a rest at the weekend, Honora pooh-poohed the idea.

'Sorcha gets plenty of rest,' Honora responded, 'and whenever she comes home she isn't in any hurry out of bed. Then she locks herself in the bathroom and runs off all the hot water.'

But everything changed when Sorcha took leave of absence from work and went to Australia. It would only be for a year she had reassured Kay.

'I'll be back,' she said. 'You won't be left with her.'

Kay knew this was not true.

'You have not the slightest intention of returning to Ireland, so you needn't pretend,' she told Sorcha, doing her best to not to envy her sister who was getting away.

'Well. . .I was thinking of organising a work permit . . .' her voice was cautious. 'But the legal end of things takes ages.'

After the first anniversary of their father's death, both Kay and Sorcha realised things had to change.

'You could come out to me, couldn't you?' Sorcha suggested on Facetime. She was sitting on her apartment balcony, smoking in the sun as she spoke.

'Like, when?' Kay sighed, watching her sister's freckled and slightly tanned face on the laptop. In the background, she noted the fronds of an exotic plant in a cinnamon-coloured urn.

Her sense of Australia was based on a few stored visions of the great Opera House, dream-songs, rich wines and the knowledge that it harboured the most poisonous arachnid population on the planet.

'Like next Christmas.'

Once that was settled, the past crept up on Kay during the summer, ambushing her with memories which told her in no uncertain terms that their mother never cared much for motherhood or marriage, despite the glowing write-up she constantly gave the latter since the onset of widowhood. The forgiving women's circles and therapeutic professionals Kay had been supported by when her attention had wandered during one quick fling with a man half her age, or when she and Pat had had to deal with their children's reading difficulties and a contrary mathematical zeal, did not exist back then. Then, parenthood was a solitary journey, all the more so after Honora and Paul decided to adopt Sorcha.

Kay was six. She recalled the day of the adoption, the trip to Dublin to the place where her new sister Sorcha Veronica awaited her. She looked forward to telling the two names of her brand-new sister the next day in school. The six-month-old wore a little white outfit with a pink and white hat. She recalled how the baby constantly clucked and fidgeted on the way home in the car, attempting to remove the hat, which Honora insisted on replacing.

Other things came later. What she remembered she now passed on to Sorcha, who had forgotten some of the episodes although she in particular experienced them when very small, things which left Kay with an unhealed atrial scar. The slappings and beatings, the cane that hung from a hook in the kitchen near the thick-planked back door, especially for disciplining Sorcha, things which still burdened Kay with the guilt only a child bystander can absorb.

The previous two festive seasons had been spent at the old family home. When it was clear that her father was in his final weeks, they had packed and driven west. In the days that followed both Kay's parents behaved garrulously, like two drunks although both were stone cold sober. The next Christmas, after Paul's death, Honora refused to come to Kay's house.

Again they drove west and spent the days with Honora, who was irritable and tearful. On the return journey, Kay's eldest son Killian demanded to know if Grandma Honora would be alive next Christmas.

Kay had smiled. 'I'm sure she will. But we won't be spending it with her.'

A sigh of approval filled the car.

Now it was late September, Kay thought that would give Honora time to adjust to the idea. Aunt Rose sat down as Honora and Kay moved around organising dinner. As usual, the plates were stacked in a pool of hot water in the kitchen sink. Kay removed each one and dried it with a dish-towel, held it out to her mother, who then served a couple of cuts of bacon, a mound of cabbage and a lake of white sauce. No matter how often Aunt Rose said 'just a little', Honora kept pouring until the food was completely bathed in thick sauce.

Kay had decided to be systematic and detached. Her mother was not the usual kind of widow, if such a category existed, easily packaged and defined, a grey-haired lady sitting in the corner knitting or taking holidays with other old people. She was fierce and alive, despite her age. Kay was determined to approach the matter lightly but firmly. Yet the fact was, she sometimes feared her mother who was a bully, who could still occasionally bring her eldest daughter to heel. She had spent her life doing that—often by mimicking Kay's voice, which was high and thin—but not to Sorcha, about whose portly child's body and short neck she would remark on as if these were defects. Sorcha no-neck, Sorcha no-neck. Sorcha always fought back, the result being that she had often been beaten or caned by Honora. Sometimes, Honora would push the child into the corner of the kitchen and take a swipe at her cheek or arm, her diamond rings occasionally grazing the skin making it bleed. Her filed fingernails would also dig into the child's shoulders. Once, in adulthood, Honora confided in an unguarded moment to Kay that she used to pinch Sorcha when she was a baby to make her cry. That Honora apparently felt guilt and remorse at this satisfied Kay. But that her mother would dare to confide such an atrocity, as if it was just any old secret, shocked and upset her. Guilt and remorse were her mother's due, she believed, distressed by this further knowledge of monstrous maternity.

As a child, Kay's resistance to Honora grew in a different way, through outward compliance and by doing what she wanted by subterfuge. She was also, she could never forget, the natural born child, the favoured one, the wise receiver of confidences. Now at forty-two she found herself in a state of constant miserable contemplation of her mother.

It would be bloody fantastic, her husband Pat encouraged, to actually be on the other side of the planet for a full month in the sun. The boys would adore the trip they both reasoned, visions of the outdoor life mounted in their heads, the notion of a Christmas beach barbecue with Sorcha, who now lived with a man she met at an AA meeting within her first week in Sydney.

That was the other legacy of Sorcha's childhood. By the time she was twenty-three she was a full-blown alcoholic and drug addict. Rehab group therapy sessions emphasised to the family that other family members were in no way responsible for the addictions of their loved ones. This gave Honora great satisfaction, Kay remembered grimly.

Why did she find it so difficult to make the announcement? If her mother were a giving sort of person, she would tell her and Pat to go off and enjoy themselves.

She took a mouthful of sauce-sodden cabbage and sat back to dredge it between her teeth.

'Dinner okay?' Honora's eyes were like picks as she fixed her with a look.

'Very tasty.'

The Capital of Outer Mongolia

'That's the last of your father's cabbage.'

Aunt Rose looked up. She was eating quietly and steadily. Now, her eyebrows crept slowly up her forehead as the surprise of it dawned on her.

'Is that the last of it? Wasn't he great, always at something!' she exclaimed.

'He was, God love him,' Honora answered, before putting down her cutlery and holding her hands to her face. Small tears spurted again. 'I used to watch the way he'd prepare it, how he'd wash every single leaf and never remove the stalks. Mind you, I like to remove the stalks, but that was his way,' she went on indulgently. 'Then he'd par-boil it before chopping. And then he'd divide it equally into plastic bags for freezing.'

'This lot's more than par-boiled.' Another mouthful of cabbage slid down Kay's throat.

'No point in eating half-raw cabbage dear, is there?'

'He actually liked it on the crisp side,' Kay went on regardless, irritated by the hagiographic element that had crept into the conversation.

Aunt Rose chipped in. 'Oh I well remember how he'd prepare the cabbage as a young boy,' she cleared her throat, wiped her lips with a napkin. 'He was always doing little chores for Mammy.' Aunt Rose smiled innocently across the table at her sister-in-law, who glared at her dinner plate and said nothing.

It was time to speak.

'I had an e-mail from Sorcha last week,' Kay began, cutting another piece of bacon.

'Good to know that you girls are in touch,' Honora replied.

'Sorcha and Peter will be spending Christmas on the beach.'

'One would expect that.' A pause. 'Of course, Sorcha never has much news. I sometimes think they have no real social life to speak of.'

Kay held her breathing steady. 'I suppose it's no better nor worse than anybody else's. It's her home now.'

'Every time I see her on the laptop screen, her skin looks very dry. That climate doesn't suit her,' Honora continued. 'And smoking cigarettes has deepened the lines around her mouth.'

Honora spooned a little more white sauce onto her cabbage, then looked at Aunt Rose, whose head, daffodil-like, was dipped towards her plate as she ate her way through hillocks of meat and liquid valleys of sauce and potato.

'As a matter of fact,' Kay continued, putting down her cutlery. Honora waited. 'We're thinking of going out there ourselves this year.'

Her mother's face remained expressionless, her feelings concealed for the first time that day.

'For Christmas, I mean.'

'So I gather,' Honora replied smoothly.

Aunt Rose looked up. 'That will be lovely for you!'

'Lovely,' Honora repeated. 'Are the flights booked?'

'I'll see to it next week.'

It all seemed remarkably easy, Kay mused. Good old Aunt Rose. Or perhaps Honora was adjusting to her new life after all. Perhaps with lessening grief a new mildness was setting in.

'I'm sure you'll enjoy yourselves,' Honora began to clear the table. Kay helped stack plates and arrange the cutlery in the dishwasher.

'Where's the cat's fork? Don't put the cat's fork in there, I keep it behind the taps,' Honora instructed.

Pudding was vanilla ice cream and freshly thawed sugared raspberries.

'I'll put coffee on,' Kay said, busying herself in the outer kitchen. In the cupboard, she found a pack of coffee. She sniffed. It was stale but she heaped four scoops into the cafetière anyway.

'You could all do with the break,' Honora resumed after swallowing a spoonful of ice cream and raspberries. She sounded almost cheerful. 'The weather will be wonderful, though the journey really is to the ends of the earth.'

'We'll probably spend a few nights in Singapore.'

'Hmm,' Honora scooped deeply into her pudding bowl.

'I suppose it will be just yourself and Aunt Rose together this Christmas then?' Kay asked tentatively.

'I don't know about that,' Honora replied.

'Thinking of inviting Uncle Jim then?' Kay speculated.

Honora looked amused.

'You can't be serious!' she chuckled with a quick shake of the head. 'No dear, I was thinking of something quite different. Now, just pulling a few thoughts together very quickly, mind . . .'

Kay waited. She imagined what her mother was going to say. That she was going to go abroad herself. She'd often mentioned how she'd like to spend Christmas in the Canaries or in North Africa or even Ethiopia. Good on her. Dame Freya Stark here we come.

Honora smiled. 'You could easily persuade me to accompany you. If you wanted a chaperone for the boys,' she broke off with a girlish laugh, 'and a surprise for Sorcha too!'

Kay stared into her pudding bowl, then lifted her head slowly. For fuck's sake. Aunt Rose silently watched mother and daughter as the conversation tacked into treacherous waters.

'Are you serious, mother?'

'I won't intrude. I can do my own thing.'

'I—I don't think—'

The Capital of Outer Mongolia

'Oh Kay, stop dithering!' Honora snapped.

'If you'd just give me a chance to—to—explain . . .' Kay stammered. Her mother was brusque again, in that intolerant way that reduced her to a state of nerves, and always had. 'What I'm trying to say is that it might be too much for you—it's a twenty-three-hour journey . . .'

'Not if you're breaking it in Singapore.'

'Even so. We'd like a family holiday this time, you know?'

'No, I don't know. Tell me,' Honora said sweetly.

'For Christ's sake, stop being a bloody bitch about everything!' Kay shouted.

Honora's eyebrows shot up to her hairline, and a vein pulsed down the centre of her forehead.

'Oh that's nice, that's lovely lang . . .'

'We want to spend Christmas by ourselves.'

'I never realised it was such a burden to you, to be here in the family home, with me and your-father-God-bless-him when he was alive. You know how highly he thought of you.'

'It is beside the point how highly he thought of me, and if he thought so highly of me there are a number of matters he might have attended to, but—'

The words were out before she could block them. Now she'd done it. She had implied a want, failure on her father's part.

'So this the heart of it? The will? Your father's last will and testament? I can't believe what I've just heard!'

'You haven't heard anything.'

'But I know what you're implying.'

'I'll never understand some of his decisions.'

'I'm sorry you feel that way about your father who idolised you. He thought the world of you. He only wanted what was best for you and your sister. Surely his will makes that abundantly clear?'

Now Kay's dander was up. Now the old rage had risen in her, from so far back it was beyond her comprehension that the entire world seemed to trust the script of Loving Mammy, Wise Daddy, Sane and Happy Children.

'Forget it,' she said sullenly. 'Just forget it.' If she spoke further she knew she might regret it. It was time to shut up and put up. The bastard had left not a penny to either of his middle-aged daughters. He had left everything to Honora.

'You mustn't upset yourself, dear,' Aunt Rose interjected gently, placing her thin hand on Kay's. 'All these things try us, and in the end they amount to nothing at all. Don't upset yourself, dear Kay. Your daddy loved you. Surely that's all you need to know?'

But it wasn't all she needed to know. She needed to know that he had deliberately selected even a small amount of money for each of his daughters, as if to say that he had remembered them and their struggles in life, that he knew what it was to work hard and make ends meet, and that they should enjoy themselves a little in his absence with even a few thousand euro. It would have cost him nothing. With a struggle, she nodded at Aunt Rose, then stanched the tears that had begun to rise at the sound of kind well-meant words.

Blinking rapidly, Kay looked into her mother's face which was ungiving and hurt and seemed also on the verge of tears.

'All I meant was, we are travelling alone,' she said quietly, changing the subject.

'So I can't come?'

The two women put away the remaining dishes in silence. Once or twice their hands accidentally touched as they loaded up the dishwasher but both recoiled as if stung. Every so often Honora shook her head.

'When I think of the way your father put you on a pedestal, you more than Sorcha, because you at least did something with your life . . .'

'Sorcha's done pretty well, all things considered.'

There. Something else was out, even if not explained. But Honora was by no means stupid.

'All things considered?' Honora pondered. Her little eyebrows shot up to her hairline again. 'I have apologised to Sorcha long ago. I've done my sorries . . .' she spoke quietly.

When the kitchen was tidy they retreated to the sitting-room and newspapers. Honora had still not solved the crossword puzzle. She had withdrawn from all unpleasantness to concentrate on the one clue that eluded her. She leaned over the atlas, magnifying glass in hand, one finger probing the undulations of Asia. Kay eyed her mother, who looked up suddenly as if feeling her stare and returned the look, expression inscrutable.

'I'd better go,' Kay eventually said.

'Whatever,' Honora replied, resuming her crossword. She turned another page on the old atlas.

'I need Mongolia . . .' she muttered. 'Will you fly across Mongolia on your way to Australia?'

'I doubt it.'

'I'm sure you'll all enjoy yourselves. I suppose Sorcha knows all about this?'

'Sorcha invited us. It'll be good to . . .'

'To what?'

'Be away,' Kay said.

'Without me, you forgot to add.'

'I'll get my things.' She wasn't going to be drawn again.

'Found it!' Honora was triumphant, finger stabbing at the word Ulaanbaatar, her mood transformed. It was as if all the preceding tension had suddenly lifted off her shoulders. 'I remember reading about that place years ago,' she said to Kay. 'The tribal kings held sway for centuries.

Horse people. Free, galloping across the grasslands, passing on songs and stories in the evenings, telling their troubles to the tribal elder—' she pulled a face, wrinkling her nose, '—drinking rancid butter-tea.'

She looked across the room to her daughter. Aunt Rose snored gently, bottom lip sucked in, then blown out as she puttered and wheezed.

'That was how to live,' Kay responded, her own mood softening.

Her mother put down her pen. 'And now we are not free,' she considered. 'Though we gallop everywhere. From here to LA, from here to Australia, from Beijing to London.'

'No, we are not free,' Kay conceded.

The day began to fade. They embraced awkwardly, not at all in the way Kay wanted.

Kay's car nosed down the avenue, beneath whispering beeches where insects hummed in the warmth. The window was open, autumnal air on her face. As she glanced back up the lawn to where the house crouched behind unruly rhododendron bushes, she recalled—as if a capsule had split open in her head—the brighter essences of childhood. All in a rush, they briefly quelled the badness, making it of less consequence. Sometimes, there had been high-whipped days of play, of freedom and exploration. Their own kind. Not like the horsemen of Ulaanbaatar whom Honora admired. Kay thought of how carefully she had to love her mother, despite the evidential horsemen of memory, galloping nightly across her brain.

5

Like Queens not Criminals

Darling one, this is what I remember. So that you know. I went as a woman of many parts. When I returned all the pieces of me were drawn into one silent pool. By then there was neither pleasure nor pain, fear nor courage.

I left on an autumn dawn. The fields were dragged with shadows, the river below the yard rushed and darted beneath the mist. The farm manager's collie sniffed at my perfume as I stepped into the car, then watched mournfully from beneath the beech hedge. In the distance lights from the M8 lit the horizon like yellow beads. I looked back once. The house blinds were drawn down as if for a death, the glasshouse crammed with tomatoes we'd forgotten to pick. The night before, the children had gone to my mother in Portlaoise. Vince drove them there while I packed my few things at home. The house was so silent as I dropped some tiny items into a small case, underwear, a nightdress, the flip-flops I used as slippers, I even remembered a small bottle of perfume I'd been saving for some time. Eau de something, no doubt.

At the airport, a taxi-driver outside the departure hall stared at us as we hugged. I tossed my head and went in. The woman at the ticket counter moaned about the dark mornings, then thanked God that at least she always missed the worst traffic. I paid for the ticket, checked in and made my way to the departure gate. Other passengers helped themselves to coffee and rolls but I sat tight.

When an officious-looking woman approached, my heart pounded. She was doing a survey. Was I a frequent air traveller? Had I chosen that particular airline because of its superior service? Did I find the fares competitive? I might have replied no, no and no, but I lied with three resounding yesses.

After take-off, I squinted down, picked out Liberty Hall, the pulsating estuary, East-Link Bridge, Dun Laoghaire harbour, then distant houses edging up into mountains. It was a cartographer's innocent dream. I thought about Vince making his way back across the Curragh.

The businessmen tucked into their bacon and sausages, then rattled their newspapers. My throat wanted to break, my eyes stinging as I made tears disappear down into their ducts. It wasn't just the radiance in the cabin the moment we rose above clouds, though that gracious lemony light may have contributed. I pictured the heaven I half-believed in, saw the souls of the dead and the unconceived romping below me on satiny cushions of light and vapour, frivolous with the wisdom of having lived and died, some of them actually waiting to come back for another go at life. Of course I tumbled into a wishful form of religion, I wanted a divine voice to urge me to change my mind. I even imagined someone calling my name, softly, with a mercy not of this earth, 'Roberta. Roberta. *Go home!*'

By the time the plane landed I felt better, even relished the chance of a day in the city. Shopping, a film—any amusement would have done. On the Piccadilly Line someone offered me a seat. I tried to settle myself, glanced around at the tightly packed standing groups, a man with a banjo, a girl with hair braided in orange and turquoise beads, then two glossy-haired women who got off at Knightsbridge. After a while the man with the banjo found a seat and began to strum quietly. Nobody looked his way, except me.

When I emerged from the underground a woman at a newsstand was helpful and knowing. She was probably familiar with Irish accents. 'Dearie', she called me in her Cockney way, and I almost crumbled on the spot, at my age, because her voice was sympathetic. She looked right at me, took her time as she told me where the street was. I hadn't slept at all the previous night.

Later that morning, I met a young counsellor who expected me to scream and shout and cry and told me not to bottle things up. Although I said little, I was sure, so very sure. My only concern was your pain. And my soul. But mainly the pain I might cause. We guessed your approximate size—similar to a 20p coin, maybe a 50p coin. Yes, a 20p English coin. Very small, the counsellor assured me.

'And now, Roberta,' an Indian doctor enquired after the medical examination, 'just what are you going to do about the state of things in your country? Can you do something for the women who cannot afford to come here?' At her words, I thought of poor X who was eventually allowed to travel, but also of the thousands of others, older than her.

The gold hoops of her earrings waggled as she spoke and her smile was good-humoured. The state of things in my country. I swear I wanted to do everything. Right then I wanted to drop a bomb on the whole island. I wished we belonged to the Brits, who would allow for some possibility of innocence and not guilt.

Half an hour later the doctor handed me the address of a safe house where I would spend the night. Outside on the street, hunger pangs rolled through me. I had to eat. In a restaurant which wasn't McDonalds but not the Dorchester either, I picked at some plaice and chips.

It consoled me to watch a young couple with their infant son. If I was looking for a sign, then this was it. The father fed him in spoonfuls and the little lad made monkey sounds for more food each time the spoon was withdrawn. Then he tilted his head back and sucked at a bottle of milk, held by his mother. The sound of his sucking got to me, became mothering lust. A perfect image of modern parenthood. Something shifted within me.

I paid up and hurried out to the nearest kiosk. I had to phone Vince. I'd fly home later that day, yes, we'd go through with the whole thing and count our blessings and hope for the best. The kids would think it marvellous. I fumbled for change but hadn't enough, then saw that it was a credit card kiosk and I had a useless Irish card which wouldn't work in London. Even our plastic didn't work. I'd left my proper cards at home, had brought only large denominations of cash to pay them at the place. For some reason that brought me to my senses. I stood a moment, sweating, the traffic lurching beside me on the road. In a split second, I knew what could be and what could not.

At the safe house I met Amber, in her sixties and used to Irish women. My age didn't surprise her. She had dogs, a cockatoo and three cats. In Victorian times, she told me, the house belonged to the local signalman. It made me think of Charles Dickens' ghost story, *The Signalman*—Vince's favourite—and about places where unaccountable things happen and good doesn't always prevail. I was certain the place would be haunted.

But my pink-walled bedroom was peaceful, had absorbed so much that it betrayed nothing. Indian brass plates and bits of carved teak hung between the ceiling and the wainscotting along the landing. In the sitting-room, aspidistras in a tangle in front of the open bay windows, coffee tables with chipped inlay, and two oil-lamps with pink globes contributed to the stillness. Outside in the garden, the wind hushed through the lofty apple trees and the sky smouldered. I felt at ease.

'Fancy some brandy, lovey? Turkey sandwiches? I'm right here if you want to talk, any time, night or day . . .' It makes me smile now to admit that I mumbled something about the soul. It was the first time I'd uttered the word. She turned and seized me by the shoulders.

'Listen to me, lovey, you're here now, and you're going out tomorrow morning for your operation. You hear me?' She peered into my face but her expression was kind.

'Yes,' I replied slowly, 'I want to.'

She smiled. 'Good. Then you'll go home and get on with your life. That's all there is to it.'

All that remained was to phone Vince. Your father. Amber showed me to a private phone cubicle off the hall. We chatted in low shamed voices.

'I've broken my specs,' he mumbled.

'I'm frightened,' I said.

'The children are fine,' he blundered on.

'Wish you could've come.'

'I know.' His voice was deep and soft. Then we both blew our noses and began to talk about schools and book lists, about milk cheques and being nearly three thousand gallons over quota.

'I'll phone tomorrow. From the place.'

'Yeah,' he said, 'Do that.'

That night the suburb was so quiet I could have been at home. Occasionally the cockatoo squawked from its cage in the hall. I knew exactly where I was, felt the distance between me and Vince, lay awake for yet another dawn.

The clinic was an ordinary pretty Arts and Crafts-style house. I hope you'll understand this, you who lived briefly. I do know something about beauty, how it lies in wait at the dark heart of our lives. The trees outside the place, lush with leaf, reminded me of the beech grove near the river, where Vince and I sometimes go after harvest; all we do is watch the light dwindle, throw sticks for the dogs, wonder about the future.

I recall a powerful tugging, not pain, for me at least. I hope it wasn't brutal for you. Afterwards the anaesthetic released despair from beneath my phoney confidence. I bawled and slobbered so much that a Jamaican nurse told me to pull myself together. I might have been eighteen instead of forty-three. But it didn't matter.

I met a married woman from Hull, and a teenager from Wales, then a single woman who worked in the City and hadn't been at work the day a terrorist bomb exploded there, and two Nigerian women. We rested that evening. We were treated like queens not criminals. I missed Vince. Most of the others had men or mothers by their beds. Later that night, our chat was cautious, but gradually our lives unravelled in long spools which would never be revealed to anybody else.

I feel no shame in the fact that a taxi whisked me away through the back exit the next morning because the protesters had arrived out front.

'Some folk don't 'ave nothin' better to do on a Saturday,' the driver remarked placidly.

In the train back to the airport, I knew I'd been delivered. I observed the English suburban gardens, brilliant berried rowan trees, small orchards, autumnal shrubs and blooms, purple or flaming; I admired the precise love of the earth which clings to city people. The truth is, I was entranced by a place like this which could forgive.

Back home, the pool of my life has deepened to something so adult and silent that nothing can threaten it. Vince booked himself in for a vasectomy. Then he wouldn't touch me for a long time, nor I him. Out of respect. Not for one another, but for you. It didn't seem right. Only a heightened conscience—or none at all—permits certain actions. And people with physical natures, which means most people, have to dice with consequences.

You didn't let go easily even if I took up the thread of my life again, was content, could laugh. Why would you? For a long time, I felt you close by. One night I got up for a drink of water, caught sight of my reflection in the long bedroom mirror, sensed a presence, a pale greyness that trailed me, as if—as if—yes, a shape and a high, small voice.

Eventually, you gave up and eased your way out. For all I know, the speck of your soul has dropped into someone else's life. Perhaps you've attached yourself already to the end of some starry-eyed kiss or promise. Perhaps you're back among us, in a tight thudding universe, orbiting upside down in the capsule of some other woman's belly, waiting. That's the thing about growth. The only option is to try again. Dear child, you will grow yourself again, I know that.

6

Peach Jam

Deborah tracked him down but did nothing about it for eight days. The tracking part was easy, even though she knew he wouldn't be on any social media. Forty years ago, he'd been a slightly old-fashioned boy, remote from the modernity that surrounded but never quite penetrated that curving thumb of the county.

But the Shunnock Harriers were on Facebook, and there it was she found him, sitting at a long table with his companions, brothers and sisters of the hunt, hands folded carelessly in his lap as he smiled at the camera.

'Is that him?' her daughter squeaked in puzzlement when she too found the photograph. She knew all about her mother's first love. So did her husband, and one of her closest friends.

'Yes. Why?'

'He looks younger than I thought he'd be.'

It was true. He'd inherited his mother's sallow skin and, although balding, looked relatively unlike many of the men she encountered on the literary circuit. They were serious men, who dressed in black or grey, whose greying tufts were dishevelled. Around them, one or two female poets revolved like small desperate moons, ambitious to avail of the gravitational pull of the already seriously successful. But Jamie was still himself, just as in brighter moments she considered that she was still herself.

Thoughts of him had come and gone over the years. There was no particular pattern, except that she dreamed of him from time to time. In the dream he was still elusive. Often the skinny little spike that had been his mother hovered in the background. But there were moments of pleasure in those dreams too. Occasionally she sat opposite him and they talked in ordinary tones, the way ordinary people talk. Of what she could never recall, even in those pre-waking moments when she could set most details of a dream in the cement of relative accuracy.

There was no reason she shouldn't try to contact him or put her forensic skills to good use. Press boundary walls. Have a secret. She was good at that. It was one thing you learned as a writer, that there were secrets everywhere to be uncovered, and that connections to the most unlikely people were rarely as outlandish as might be imagined.

There had been occasions when she had driven the road past his house, an early 19th century manse with a little stone bridge at the entrance. It might be described by a word nobody used anymore unless in an estate agent's description: picturesque. The bridge was the right width for the horses and carriages that had crossed it throughout the nineteenth century and probably into some of the twentieth. Before the motorcar. Before the roads around the nestling town were widened, trimmed and marked, before land was purchased from farmers and straighter, less sunken roads allowed vehicles to snort and zoom from glen to shore and back again.

She could never resist slowing down as she approached the town, and it had nothing to do with speed limits. She was intent on peering in across that bridge, to see if a light was on in the cottage, or if she could spy a shape moving within, or perhaps she might see him outside, leading a horse to a stable followed by brown pointers with taut electric tails. But not once had she seen him in forty years of passing along that road from time to time. Probably no more than twenty times, she reckoned, mostly when she was coming to, or leaving, the artist's colony known as 'Retreat by the Loch' five miles away. If she was coming, she was excited at the prospect of peace and concentration. If she was departing, it was a question of carrying her new trove—a treasure, sometimes hard won—and bearing the precious load home to her own household, across the Sound some eighty miles distant. On arrival, waves of affection, of delight, would engulf her. The dogs also sensed the return of an absent prodigal figure and the air of incipient celebration when her husband put a leg of Highland lamb in the oven and her daughter made lemon tarts. But it was not easy to hold onto the dispassion of the writing, and she did not find in her own study the haven of steady outpouring that she felt in Retreat by the Loch. There was nobody to blame but herself.

But she did wonder if she and Jamie could ever have a conversation again. If it would be possible. What, she wondered, might he have learned? It was not possible to reach his age and not have learned a thing or two. And had she learned anything? After all, why would she want to reopen this aperture to the past? She had learned a lot, mostly through her bullish tendency to make things difficult for herself, by being full of pride and seeking attention and reward through her cleverness. Unable to be a sycophant, she had learned much about the operations of society.

So what would it cost her if she was to break fences for a change? It was high time she unearthed the most important thing of all at this moment, undertook a probe that was part curiosity and part obsession. Her mother used to call her an oddity because she was shy as a girl and avoided talking to people on the street or on the telephone. She was so shy that she preferred winter to summer, because in winter she felt a little more invisible and could slink along the inside of a street without being called out to by anybody. But now she could cross a room in any town, city or country and speak to anybody. She no longer feared the telephone, or not knowing what to say in the right way. Crowds could not intimidate her when she had to address them at readings and lectures. She had all her words, lined up to such fluency that a book dedication to her from another writer was once addressed *To Deborah, who is never lost for words.* And although she briefly considered that the writer may have intended a note of irony in the inscription, on balance she took it as well meant.

This would be her journey. This was yet another private time. She could do what she damn well liked. She was due to cross the Sound on the ferry and drive back to the writers' retreat for a month. Perhaps then she might risk something. She opened up her laptop and surveyed the Facebook page. He seemed unperturbed, gentle-looking, a little impenetrable. Quickly she enhanced the image so that it was clearer, clicked Save, then lifted her head away from the screen and gazed out the window, where house martins swung in and out of a terrace of nests beneath the eaves. The window ledge was spattered with droppings.

During the weeks away, she worked on an early draft of a novel. The place was packed. Painters, writers, one sculptor and three musicians all met up in late afternoon to swim in the loch or go boating. Sometimes people brought wine and sandwiches. There was talk of publishers and agents and envious chat about advances, although everybody declared that the age of the six-figure advance was dead and buried.

While she worked she never thought of Jamie. She'd hunted him down without his knowing it, like a fox that had eluded her all these years, and that brought a certain satisfaction. And she'd hunt him further yet. It was a question of nerve and of holding it. Six years older, he'd thought so little of her, drawn to her initially because of her resemblance to a woman some years older than himself who had rejected him. He'd insisted to Deborah that she wasn't yet a woman, that she was still a girl, something which had deeply wounded her. As they drove out at nights in his Cavalier Coupé, tearing along the switchback roads towards discos on both sides of the Sound, but mostly on her side, she knew she didn't understand the rules of the county game. She didn't get it that all she had to do was be hard and ungiving, to hold herself back instead of allowing him to kiss her so that she was in a frenzy for him. He was the first man to reveal his cock to her. She ate, slept and drank thoughts of him. Not that sleeping came into it, because she ceased to sleep, or at best slept brokenly, the mere whisper of him in a dream awakening her before dawn when daylight would disturb her and she felt sick in her stomach.

She broke from work one early afternoon and took a walk around the loch. All the painters were still in their studios, and most of the writers still sat at their laptops in the quandary of invention and lying that marked their hours. There were the usual fishermen, perched at intervals along the shore, their boxes of bait—maggots, worms and fancier artificial coloured insects—lying open to the elements. On the hill opposite, the forest that had crowded up along its incline over the past thirty years was now being felled and the drone of mechanical saws rose and fell across the still waters. It was said that the pine martens which had been repopulating the area would retreat and be lost. Rain had fallen and her boots squelched as she passed along the broken path. She'd always loved this part of the county. It was as rich and earthy as she could ever have wished for, so it was all the more strange to her sometimes that she had chosen to live away from it all, in a very flat area liable to be flooded with the waters of the Sound in spring and autumn, without the crowding presence of woodlands and the plushness of wild birds and craggy-pathed inaccessible lakes that nobody wanted to swim in or develop. But she had chosen to live with a man who was good for her. He was like a deep wave begun far out at sea, supporting her with his depths and his tides, accompanying her to any shore she would land on.

It came to her suddenly, the simplest thing. There was no point turning up at Jamie's doorway unannounced. She could have done that. The only thing to do was to write him a note. Put it in an envelope, so that no nosy parker could read its innocuous contents. She stopped dead in her tracks, astounded by the level of her own premeditation. She must be mad. She was mad, a fully-fledged grown-up oddity, just as her mother had predicted. She would be like this till the day she dropped which, she assumed, would probably be sometime within the next twenty-five years. It would be ridiculous not to write.

She lifted her right foot then and withdrew it from the mud and matted grass into which it was sinking. *Schloop, schloop* went her two feet. She turned. A wood pigeon battered its way out of the forest and across her path, honking in alarm. The shoreline shivered in the lightest of breezes.

She drove into the town to buy a postcard. The local newsagents was closed for refurbishment. Already, she could see the brand-new Victorian pastiche look that was half installed. In the supermarket she drifted through disorganised narrow aisles, but it did not bother her. At the card stand she took her time scrutinising the different categories. His. Hers. Mother. Father. Engagement. Wedding. Congratulations. It was hard to find an uncategorised card, impossible to find a plain postcard. She should have gone to the post office, she realised too late, selecting the plainest card she could find. It showed an image of the town at the turn of the previous century. Black and white, with an envelope. It was a beautiful image, showing the wide town square and courthouse, and a few people crossing it—women in Edwardian style and hats, men also wearing hats, a resting horse and cart outside a public house. She had often wanted to live in another time, to be there in person, to know and smell and feel the air and the sweat and the life around her. How hard she had sometimes found it to do such things in her own time.

She replaced the black and white image on its stand. The post office would have what she was looking for. She left the car in the supermarket car park and walked up the hilly street, to the crest, where a café door lay open and the smell of coffee wafted out. Her stomach rumbled. She would call in there on her way back.

The post office interior was modernised, although the exterior was still distinctly of its time, and local-looking. Inside an efficient young woman was dealing with the small queue of five women. Three of them were Roma; a grandmother, mother and daughter. She knew such people were housed in what was once a local agricultural college but which she really knew was a human zoo for immigrants that the government didn't know what to do with. The grandmother looked completely uncomprehending. One of the others was a diminutive Philippina teenager. The woman ahead of her was, she thought by her accent as she chatted on her mobile phone, from the islands beyond the Sound. It was not a pension or welfare day because the queue moved swiftly while she perused the stand of postcards. She flicked along the scenic images of the county and found what she was looking for. A plain white rectangular card whose only message would be contained in her writing. Postage was already included on this particular type of card, so she paid and moved to a side counter.

For a moment, she thought about leaving to head for the cafe in order to write the card, but dismissed the idea. This had to be done quickly but carefully. Strategy yet not strategy. Who was she fooling? She did not use the post office pen, a biro with a half-broken plastic shaft from which leaked thick blue ink, and withdrew her own chubby 0.5 black Uniball Stilo.

Dear Jamie,

This will seem like a weird blast from the past, after forty years. I've occasionally passed your house, usually on my way from Retreat by the Loch, and wondered how you've been and what you are up to. I heard your mother had died—sincere sympathies on her death—

At this, she smiled. His widowed mother, her haughty clinging disposition, had been his problem. She had reined him in as tightly as necessary to bend him into believing that staying at home was best. That was what she, Deborah, had once believed. She also assumed that—provided he remembered her—he would know what had become of her, well-known writer and cultural commentator that she was, and would therefore understand why she might be staying in Retreat by the Loch. She continued her note.

My own mother, though frail, is still alive, which means I'm in the area every two weeks or so. I was wondering if you'd like to meet up sometime for coffee or a drink? That's if you remember me! My number is—

Her absolute belief in the rightness of this gesture regardless of the outcome grew with every stroke of the pen.

If you feel like it, give me a call. If not, there's no problem. Best wishes,
Deborah Ross

When she left the post office, she headed for the café. Inside were a few women and two men. The men sat alone, one of them turning pages of *The Sun* while the other stared blankly ahead, one of his large hands curled around a steaming mug. She ordered a double espresso and a glass of tap water. Then, on second thoughts, a croissant with butter and peach jam.

If he ignored the postcard, she had still done something, had broken the paralysis of thought that had nagged her over the years. Then she changed her mind. You stupid woman, she now recriminated herself. And she changed it yet again. If he looked at the card in bafflement and had to struggle to remember who the hell she was, it would be worth it. But that he would remember, there was not the slightest doubt in her head. Her cousin had told her he'd once said he was sorry for how he'd treated her. So, clearly, he had not forgotten the slim girl who became a walking bag of nerves under the careless tutelage of his kisses. There had apparently been rules but she did not know them. For most people, she learned that love, though fine, was not enough and there were other considerations and things to be proven.

So she had written to him. He could laugh or he could tear it up. He could forget about it. She imagined the card discarded on a kitchen table beneath a week's newspapers and invoices. If he read it, her words would be crystal clear, unless he was an idiot, which she did not believe he was. As she buttered the croissant, she replayed in her head the moment the card had dropped into the brass postbox. It had flown from her fingertips, she had felt electricity within her own body as if her fingers were hot sparking transporters of energy, casting heat into the ether of another person's existence. She sipped her coffee, wiped her lips with the paper napkin, and added peach jam to the croissant. Then she opened up her phone to consider his face, as he gazed at a camera that had captured him and his companions.

Innocence itself, that's what he was. That was what thrilled her.

7

THE SPACE BETWEEN LOUIS AND ME

I think of Louis as a decorative essential. He doesn't do much around the place beyond being there as much as I want. He doesn't cook or clean up and can't make a bed to save his life. I watch in frustration as he goes through the motions of holding a book, knowing reading is beyond him. Yet guided by me, conversation is lucid. He is by no means stupid.

Most mornings I'm alone again. He has slipped away although he's with me until sleep falls through the dizzy mire of my semi-aroused thoughts. Nights are dreamless places where I wallow in oblivion. When I open my eyes, unrefreshed, occasional sunshine hacks through the window blind, or I hear the swat of a wet westerly on the glass. I am persistently exhausted, though often happy.

At the clinic, a few male colleagues share my secret. The exhausted prematurely wrinkled bags beneath eyes, and that five o'clock unshaven look at nine a.m. arouse my curiosity. As if they can't be bothered keeping up appearances with basic grooming that, until recently, drove this city to a crescendo of open nail bars, high-end barber shops and massage parlours.

In general, my women colleagues are discreet. There's no knowing who or what is observed across desks and filing cabinets as we prepare for another day of group work, as we assemble files, then check our pockets for antacid supplies: Bisodol and Gaviscon.

Birchwood, as the clinic is called, is littered with divorced social workers and therapists on the move, shaking themselves free of past lives, attempting reincarnation. Such hurry! Yet apart from the usual sour clichés about *that sad fuck* and *I'll see him in court again* or even *bastard needn't think he's having the children all summer*, there isn't much talk about what's happening now. About hopes and dreams. In a way, they are as private as me. They are also too burdened, between caseloads and new admissions; the constant stream of alcoholics, gamblers and narcotics abusers housed beneath the clinic's ill-repaired roof.

I've gleaned from the whispering gallery of the coffee queue though, that some have quick flings. Others date more cautiously. One or two discovered they were gay and are in that vivid state of fresh exploration usually found with first love.

At lunchtime, while the addicts are enjoying an organic energy-optimising lunch, I sometimes walk along the estuary, past gleaming, award-winning bridges, beyond the disused gantry and the giant upside-down question mark of an orange hook that dangles in the gap between the struts. The air is briny. Blindfolded, you'd think you were on a daytrip to the seaside, but with eyes wide open this river is oily and sluggish, pouring itself like green ink into Dublin Bay. Gulls scream around the few docked ships, metal screeches and groans at a nearby foundry. There's no chance I'd run into Louis. Impossible in fact. His very existence, boastful though it sounds, depends on me. This knowledge lends me no satisfaction.

I once observed someone else in the same situation as myself. Near the train station, a man who might have been on his way back to an office, hung around beneath the huge round clock as passengers streamed in and out, their jackets flapping in the wind. At two minutes past two in the afternoon there he was beneath the black Roman numerals chatting to himself. The average passer-by might assume he was speaking into a discreet mouthpiece, or that he belonged to the scattering of walking talking mad who traverse the city, especially in winter. But it was more than that. He adjusted his spectacles then a tiny ear-piece. Anyone would assume he was near-sighted and slightly deaf.

Working with addicts fucks up the most balanced disposition, although that's not my excuse. The Serenity

Prayer isn't all it's cracked up to be either. You ferret out what makes life bearable. Some convince themselves work is the key. They become top salespeople or even middling salespeople, or they build credits doing self-improvement courses. Others, like me, travel as often as they can manage it. I'm entitled to seven weeks' holidays plus a week's sick leave. Not bad. I once committed myself to evening car maintenance, became quite chummy with the under-the-bonnet fumblers, all male, then gave up. Useful as it is to understand the workings of the average car engine, points and plugs didn't really sail my boat. Then came wine tasting, sausage making, cheese making, Italian, and a series of art history lectures. All sublimation, the lot of it.

As I can't spend my entire life with Louis, work at the clinic fills time between breakfast and evening. It pays the bills. Coffee's good too. I achieve some successes with the depraved and broken, am acknowledged to be kick ass but not cruel. The only thing that riles me is when Significant Others remain enablers, making excuses, slipping bottles of gin, little pick-me-ups that interfere with the work. As a result I've deleted my share of abusive e-mails. Once or twice on the phone, I've had to cut off the parent of some pasta-faced heroin-addicted daughter or son in mid-rant. An upset alcoholic pregnant woman once screamed herself hoarse in group, the child she was carrying already a pickled walnut. This is abnormal, but in the circumstances also normal. An alcoholic cartoonist with a stammer that made him sound even more aggressive, who never quite kicked his gambling habit, also made a regular nuisance of himself by writing me poisonous unwelcome love letters.

But a heavy caseload doesn't mean I don't read and write. Call me an artist *manqué*, I know how to look, how to look again, how to reread. I have drawers filled with notebooks bought in galleries around the world. Snapshut magnetic covers, embroidered covers, lined, unlined, Moleskine, Chinese, Quaderno, wood-pulp, school jotters, filled with wandering words from the bird in my chest. My yellow-bricked apartment overlooking the canal is sanctuary to bird-words, to many necessary fripperies trawled home from the world beyond our island. It satisfies me to wear a moonstone ring and imagine it was given to me, that Louis gave it to me when in fact this would be impossible, because he has no money, no currency. It excites me to warm a chained oblong of tiger's eye in my hand before draping it on my breastbone, the chill gone. I imagine his honey-coloured hand warming it, not mine. Sometimes too, I dance before him, in the bedroom, enveloped in a length of rose madder silk from the province of Uttar Pradesh.

In India I managed without Louis. I made a pact with myself for strength in the face of temptation. In fairness, he did not ask to come. Before I left I enquired casually if he would miss me.

'Of course I'll miss you,' he replied with annoying equanimity. But self-control is his middle name. This is how he came to me. Poised, quietly confident but capable of submission to my will, my harmless needs. A woman couldn't ask for more.

'How much will you miss me,' I pressed.

He turned with a radiant smile and answered with open arms, 'I will miss you to the floors of the oceans and the roof of the skies.'

Poetic, eh? I continued packing t-shirts and loose linen trousers.

'I'll see you when I get back,' I told him in a business-like way.

'That's fine Molly. I'll be waiting. I am yours, all yours.'

Not what I was used to hearing from men. Despite myself I looked up and gazed adoringly at him. He is beautiful, from the rich tumble of brown curls on his golden neck, to the wide-set blue eyes. I wanted to bite the generous sculpt of his mouth, to softly press teeth close to blood.

One thing I've learned in the long heated therapy sessions, is that women living with men find it all a bit conditional. There's a great deal of sheet, jeans and towel folding at weekends, toilet cleaning, swanky 'couples'

The Space between Louis and Me

meals to be prepared. The middle classes can hold their own anytime when it comes to contributing to national addiction stats. Especially at Birchwood. No doubt the chaps feel the same. Resentful and obliged.

I could never have married.

When I was a child, our farm fed eleven of us. But the barrage of cousins, aunts, uncles, the annual births, the smell of plastic mugs, the metal buckets of steeping nappies conveyed a message to me. It was carried by a bird that dived into my chest like a kingfisher into a pool one night as I leaned out over the window ledge at the age of thirteen, listening to a cow lowing in the byre, smelling the lonely cold manurey air, thinking that if I could fly in a straight line over the hills I'd be in America and would end up in Los Angeles where the real stars glowed. I absorbed the bird-message, heard the high-pitched whistle of Never! Never!

That feathered little creature has never deserted me. I imagine a small Byzantine bird not from the world of nature at all, but art. Now I am fifty-one and feel the downturn of my life, the change that comes when you know the high days have passed but the cleated warmth of the afternoon is yet to be absorbed. Now I really need art.

The only one who understood how I felt was Roza. I'm proud of her; the abstract painter whose husband pushed her to sign in for six weeks' detox. She arrived into the group—puffy-skinned and sullen—but gradually open. She was able to utter the words and mean them, the flaky sentence every stand-up comedian jokes about: 'My name is Roza and I'm an alcoholic.' Most clients glare into the middle distance and slip it out quickly, but she held my gaze. After detox, she underwent the full programme, then returned home to Cork to try her luck.

We stayed in touch, had miraculous relieving telephone conversations late at night about our situations. Hers, married and too wealthy for the good of her art. Mine, single and perhaps too comfortable and intolerant for the good of my heart, and I don't mean cholesterol. Somehow, I never met the right man. Now. I've uttered it, that vile old-fashioned phrase!

I had to do something.

'What's to do,' Roza used to say in despair.

'There must be something,' I'd reply with a sigh from my king-sized cloudy-duveted bed, smoking weed. By this stage, the professional distance necessitated by her stay at the clinic had long dissolved.

'Face it girl,' she'd reply, 'we're up the creek without a paddle, we're gettin' old.' Her Cork accent made it all seem much more desperate and tragic.

Sometimes, I wept with frustration. Life stretched ahead, filled with more art and more travel, with superficial encounters, with the admiring looks of Middle

Eastern men, of Indian men, of any man who thinks a blonde Western woman is a slut. None of that was enough.

In this city, women outnumber men. But young women have the chutzpah, the oestrogen-plump looks, and until recently they had the money to pick and choose, despite the imbalance.

'We've got to do something radical,' I suggested.

'Like what,' Roza drawled cynically.

'Leave it with me,' I said.

'Wicked,' she replied.

We didn't communicate for a few weeks afterwards. I think Roza had given up, that she had almost—but not quite—decided to live the *entente cordiale* that was her uninspiring marriage, to imagine some kind of passion for the sake of her art.

Being an intensive Sunday newspaper reader turned the situation around. It takes up most of my day, whether in bed, or later in Café Lumière, near the canal bridge where the swans throng. The café door is open regardless of the weather. In winter I muffle up inside, newspaper supplements spread, a large coffee steaming to my right. At other tables, couples and young families are out for a lazy breakfast. An Irish fry-up or waffles and honey. Outside, greedy swans close in, frothing and jostling on the trim grassy bank, heads rising and dipping. I perused the Personals page for a few moments before zooming in on something. I spent a good few minutes reading and rereading. It wasn't the usual smarty-pants approach *(Cobalt blue eyes, bronze hair and a heart of gold, but also nerves of steel! M, 50)* that tries too hard *(Pineapple seeks cheese with own stick. F, 33)* to impress *(Reactive lady, 41, seeking generous physics man to 50)*.

> *Do we ever know what we're seeing? Can we ever truly touch those closest to us? Interested in experimenting with an exciting new way of seeing the man or woman of your dreams? Want to meet that man or woman? We guarantee you will not be disappointed! See the many testimonies to this exclusive Innovative Relationship Solution. Box no. 23/01*

*

I followed it up, and so did Roza. It's more difficult for her. How often can she have a new lover right there in the house with an observant amiable husband already on her case? Going out can be awkward in her suburb where even the dogs in the street would notice something amiss and bark in their best Cork accents.

The Space between Louis and Me

The people at *Rel-aid* assessed our requirements. They listened, they observed and they matched. I paid for both of us by credit card. Dissatisfied customers are refunded in full. I don't imagine there are too many. What arrived by FedEx more than met my wildest imaginings. Roza had no complaints either, has created a routine that works for her, mostly in her studio surrounded by acrylics and sandpaper.

I had no idea how closely I could observe Louis as I used *The Virtual Rel-aid* superfine goggles and minuscule ear-piece. Every pore of his skin, every small hair behind the shells of his ears, his beautiful neck, his startling golden-brown eyes were *real*. I programmed him to respond to his name, after a travel writer I admire. To refer to 'programming' is to defile him. But certain basics are required.

Louis will age as I age, keeping pace, seeing me as ever-young without actually thinking about it. He can never observe my delicate pink pallor, the gradual dissipation of my once-serene skin, nor the little cloven hoof-print of my cunt within its silvering fleece. And although I can't say he actually brings me breakfast in bed on a Saturday morning, he does stand by my shoulder when I've arranged everything on a tray. The chartreuse-coloured coffee cup, saucer and plate. Lemon-toast and one croissant. A fill of steaming Java. Two nectarines. Vitamin E.

Then he moves up the stairs ahead of me as I bear tray to bedroom, always in my field of vision. He must be straight ahead of me or slightly to the right or left. Once I move ahead he vanishes.

As I eat, he sits on the bed or stretches out beside me. He is weightless, like a feather, despite the solid bulk of his toned body. It looks as if his body is sinking deep beside me. But when I remove the goggles, the duvet is as smooth as ever, unmarked by the heft of his shoulders and the smooth curve of his ass-cleft.

I wish I could introduce him after work, in the wine bar, where I don't drink wine, but tonic and cranberry with ice. The goggles aren't all that different from ordinary spectacles and I don't look like a firefighter or someone entering a nuclear meltdown zone. The controls are subtle. Even so, I recognised them on that man outside the train station. Those in the know—vulnerable, even ashamed—are on nodding terms. A colleague from what we call the Dice Room chats as if he has known me for years. All very casual. Weather talk. Gambling gossip. The boss's latest staff restructuring scramble. Health cutbacks, indigent gamblers who are still indigent, the coked-up, the fuckem-and-forgettem in thrall to booze. Yet more health cutbacks.

Louis understands the mathematics of a broken economy. 'There there,' he says, reaching for my hand (although he'll never touch it). 'Things will get better darling. Tokyo is improving my love, and the Nasdaq's on the rise, my sweet. The HSE will provide the funds, you'll see. You'll feel better tomorrow.'

What he fails to grasp is that although the economy might improve in a few years and the paranoic addicted recover, things will not get better between him and me. We are defined by the space between us. We can never ever touch.

He cannot know that when I lie back, fascinated and wild at the sight of a *Pre-select-for-Size* erection, imagining his touch as he sits on a canary-yellow linen chair opposite my bed, that I need to believe his lustful and loving endearments, the quiet sibilance of what he enjoys most. But despite my best efforts, I'm doomed to an atheism which cannot blindly accept the myth-like advantages of modern solitude. From the bed beyond Louis's head I see the canal, frowning and purple in the wind, the swans snowy, and a trail of pedestrians hurrying home to their mysterious lives. At such moments, I sometimes remember all eleven of us children in the house on the farm; the rooms in apple greens and tropical sunset reds painted by our crazy mother, the outhouses kept distempered by our practical father. Eleven was a community. We would kneel during Lent for the rosary, always together, secretly fooling our way through all those Hail Marys. Then our parents would suddenly forget, opening a bottle of stout or a new novel (or both), switching on the television, and gradually we'd be back to our fairly secular un-rosaried domestic habits. Eleven then. Now I am one. I am not even one of two.

 I think I love Louis. I permit myself to love the presence of an absence. Provided I keep the goggles on, he's with me night and day. But they often slip off in the dreamless night. No amount of strong elastic keeps them on. Come morning, I am alone again. There will always be that space between Louis and me. But the next time I travel he's coming too. I will wrap the goggles in a blouse and place them deep in my luggage. He will exclaim at the India I know, will soak up, in his way, the intense blue of the houses of Jodhpur viewed from Mehrangarh Fort, he will fear for the children of Mumbai, and he too will move on, on, always slightly ahead, through the crowds, past the starved cows, pausing as I pause beside a kneeling astrologer in saffron-yellow who will tell my future.

8

The Stolen Man

He has already experienced eight months of horizontal winds roaring inland from Galway Bay. It suited him to rent this place, six miles distant, partly to avoid the proximity of constant celebration and the diddle-di-dye sounds that pervade the city and student life at Galway University, partly to avoid having to look too many people in the eye, such is his sense of shame.

The blackthorn hedges on the fort have finally bloomed, curbed by a mean spring that refuses warmth despite lengthening days. Every morning after waking he watches first light seeping through a dense weave of thin branches in the next field, dew-gripped stems haloed in mist.

He gets along fine with the others in his writing group on the MA programme and likes most of the tutors, although he wonders about the blonde one—the 'multi-genre writer' according to her website. It's true he's not widely read. Despite that, he was accepted as a mature student onto the creative writing course. The tutor's face had held its polite expression when he announced in class that he hadn't read many women writers apart from a few pages of one of his ex-wife's Rachel Cusks. He informed her that his favourite writers told solid stories with a beginning, a middle and an end. Hemmingway for example, he added. He shrugged as a few gentle titters rose in the seminar room then apologised for the omissions in his reading. The tutor smiled grimly and said, 'Sure we'll get you into the loop Karl, no worries, I'll have you reading all kinds of material before the year's out.' Then, a slight toss of her head and the merest (disquieting) hint of a wink.

Apart from the course, being in the rented house is another pleasure. It helps him forget, even a little. He loves returning in the evening with his groceries: fish, lentils, spinach, eggs, milk, spuds. He's trying out a life that involves a foray towards vegetarianism (but he allows himself fish), and feels the better for it. That, and walking miles around the streets of Galway after the seminars, over the bridge as the Corrib rages beneath, and later on venturing out into the vast beckoning of the fields and thready roads around his new home. The house is set in its own wilderness, on a road off the M6, with only himself and a few flapping herons from the lake below the fort.

Whether his sense of expansion derives from simply being away from Dublin for a year, feeling uncommitted and by himself, or whether it's because of the change of diet, remains to be seen. He doesn't believe in lifestyle solutions. At forty-nine, he has incipient man-breasts, thin legs and no buttocks to speak of. He's not one of those guys who drift around with a sheaf of poems sticking out of the jacket pocket or who carries a Boxer pup as a babe magnet. He consoles himself that at least he has hair he thinks of as Viking. Abundant and auburn.

The sense of renewal might also be due to the stimulation of the course, and the constant anxiety about turning in new fiction every single week to his blonde tutor. The thing that bothers him is the struggle to write out of what she calls 'the in-between spaces of experience, or liminality', another word that's bandied around a lot.

One of the other tutors is renowned for his verbal public flayings of students whose non-fiction memoirs aren't up to scratch, and he creates a terrifying presence in the classroom. A broad-shouldered, brown-haired, long-eared chap whose essays appear frequently in a big-wig journal called *Granta*. Nothing the students write can meet a standard so high Karl thinks it must give the guy altitude sickness. Long Ears doesn't believe in praising the positive and not over-emphasising the negative. They are all eejits and incompetents, with no hope of making it in the world of writing.

In the presence of Long Ears, some of the younger guys sweat. The women seem more able for him. He's pretty free with his language too. Wanker. That fuck. Oh for fuck's sake. Dropped from his mouth as a matter of course, although Karl too has begun to use similar language as he moves around the house, knocking into things when he's drunk too much at night, even more so when he has to re-draft his work.

He has discovered oxygen blowing into him after ten years in the planning offices. There was safety, yes. Collegiality yes. Green plants shivering beneath the AC system in summer as he and the others worked through the applications, assessing, budgeting. But the magisterial nature of decision-making had begun to drain him and he felt the ancient pull of wanting distance. Urgently. It has been a quest for great plains, something new to pit himself against, especially since the break-up.

The rental house with its pastiche half-door is so far removed from everything he'd known before. The one he lived in—before his marriage went pear-shaped and Anna announced that she was bisexual and had met someone else—was very different.

'You mean you're gay,' was his stunned response.

'No, I mean I'm bisexual, Karl. Bisexual? If you can take that on board.'

That really raised his hackles, apart from the shock of it. Splitting hairs, trying to have it every way. She was leaving him for another woman, so how the fuck did that make her bisexual? Was she leaving the door open, in case she changed her mind and wanted to get back with him, or be with another man?

Their home had been neat and modern. Neutral furnishings with the odd flash of a tangerine or turquoise cushion. The usual kitchen island—that oversized lump of granite, a prerequisite in every Irish kitchen when someone decided that food preparation must be performed on a space perched at a measured ratio to cooker and sink. He'd always wanted to move away from Dublin, with its constant aspiring and *garden-trimming-coordinated-fucking-furniture-Leaving-Cert-parental-helicopter-dinner-party* ambition, have a larger house, live more cheaply. But Anna wouldn't budge from chichi Portobello, by the Grand Canal, to be precise. And then she met Henni from Finland.

It wasn't like the old days when you stuck it out and put up with one another until the man died and the wife entered a new phase of doing what she pleased: bridge, hiking (that made him laugh, thinking of all the under-exercised flesh staggering up the Sugar Loaf mountain), new degree courses, and weekend breaks to Kerry. The stomach-sickening, pile-driving shock of discovering that she loves—absolutely loves—a woman, pretty much in the way she'd once loved him, took some digesting. He developed palpitations and irritable bowel syndrome, found himself dashing desperately to the bathroom to shit his guts out, all because of heartbreak. Now he was truly emptied and his heart was just beginning to grow numb, scab over. Since taking up with Henni, Anna has been having weekly therapy, suggesting in an email that he should try it too.

But for now, a house in the west. A refurbished two-hundred-year-old cottage extended to three times its original length, the original thatch replaced by a cobalt slate roof, catching every loop of light when clouds break and sunlight flashes through. The sash windows are small with bright red frames. The owner of the house, Patrick Tuomey, keeps specimen hens and cocks himself, he tells Karl, bringing him one evening to see them. They cross the yard from Tuomey's house to the white outbuildings which house the fowl.

'We have to watch out for our old friend Reynard,' Patrick had said.

When Karl looked blank, he added in Gaelic, 'An sionnach?' Still no response. Finally, exasperated, 'the friggin' fox?'

Karl leant to inspect the huge fluff-legged ruddy-feathered cocks with trembling combs and fierce eyes that burned at him in an apparently irritated way. Patrick said strangers upset them, and it was true judging by the rumpus and squawking up and down the separate coops. A

The Stolen Man

massive specimen with loosely bobbing blue-green plumes on its tail eyed Karl before dropping a generous shite. Then it strutted around, red comb wobbling in a way he found slightly repulsive. The bird also reminded him of a judge entering court, disregarding the minions.

'If he was mine I'd call him Judge,' Karl said absently.

'His name is Seamus,' Patrick replied softly as if reading his mind, opening the pen and reaching in to fondle the bird.

*

Karl's long bedroom is at the west wall of the cottage, and from the bed he can watch the evening light and the fairy fort in the field. It is ringed by gnomish blackthorn trees, their leaves sometimes glossed by moonlight. In the middle an ancient oak tree thrusts gnarled branches over the blackthorn. Patrick had warned him the previous autumn that he might see people coming and going.

'It's a fairy fort,' he emphasised, 'so they won't ever set foot on it, they're just leaving offerings.' There were two reasons, he went on. Stillborn babies, buried long ago outside church grounds, but also the presence of the Little People themselves, the *Sidhe*, or fairies. 'Arra, it's a local thing. No man will plough that fort. It isn't done.'

Occasionally he brought a few folklorists to the site.

Some afternoons as he sits at the kitchen table, laptop open, struggling to grasp Michel Foucault's theories, he raises his head to see two or three people walk past the house. Women, mostly, though not entirely. They bear bunches of daffodils. He finds it incredible, this carapace that resists modernity, the laying of scraps of ribbon on branches, licking tongues of colour in the breeze, all for the sake of maintaining diplomatic relations with the other world he only half-believes in.

He strides along the periphery of the field from time to time, sticks to the hawthorn and ash surrounds. Occasionally he approaches the mound. It reminds him of a book his sister had when they were children which showed the Little People trooping back inside their secret kingdom. Another picture illustrated marvellous times within the fort, with handsome adult fairies dancing together in an eternal state of joyous youth, while their tender children pranced in circles of their own. But sometimes they stole a living child leaving a changeling in its place, dead forever to its grieving parents. At this memory, he feels uneasy. Back then, a constantly disagreeable or tearful child might be called a changeling by its frustrated angry mother or father.

One night, he again considers that sense of unease. He was not a tearful child himself. He smiles into the dark above his bed when suddenly a face-drenching wave of self-pity sweeps through him as he recalls the trials of the past two years, knowing himself to have been abandoned by his wife. But it's the final week of semester. There are poems to hand in and twenty-five pages of memoir. He must get a grip, forget his wife. There will be divorce papers, and soon.

Kiki, a Greek woman in the memoir group, has advised him to focus on a primary incident, such as his feelings about his wife leaving him. She knew about that, because it had tumbled out in a sweaty moment of revelation during a seminar on female identity and transgressive responses, which garnered him unasked-for sympathy, empathy and all shades of feeling in between. He has taken her advice and written freely. His vocabulary might not be the most scholarly but by now he believes he has something to say.

It hasn't been easy. Remembering one particular party, an after-work thing of Anna's to which he'd been invited. To think he'd been there on the very night she'd met this Henni girl. And that is what he writes about. Blindness (his). Unknowingness (his). The sounds of a Harcourt Street summer evening, of trams rumbling along outside, and within the pub the voices of Anna's female office colleagues. Writing this piece of personal revelation causes him to weep again, but in the end he submits the work, Student ID at the top of the document.

After submitting two of his three papers, relief flows. Kiki has just completed hers, so has Paulo, from Brazil. They retreat for a coffee to the colourful student café, Bialann, with its vibrant vegetarian choices, and fling their bags to the floor. He has adjusted to this seething world of youthful bodies and understands the relative ease of being largely invisible. Kiki and Paulo, and a Belfast girl with a speech impediment, are gentle good-humoured company. The Belfast girl writes sensitive lyric poetry which, when she reads it, emerges from her mouth in a rockfall of strangulated language. She too is alone he senses. He wouldn't mind taking his chances with her but knows she'd consider him a fucking fossil.

He sips his coffee and lets the chit-chat wash softly over him. Occasionally he chips in with a riposte or a comment. Paulo is dismissing various theories about gender, flinging his arms in the air. 'What about racial identity,' he demands. This sets Kiki off and an argument ensues.

That afternoon he drives home slowly. With three weeks to work on his final manuscript, he has already half-assembled three short stories. Enough time perhaps to invent and draw another down from the clouds.

He drops the car keys on the kitchen table and decides to have a lie-down. The luxury of acting on occasional tiredness is new. The afternoon is warm, the sun flings light across the unmade bed, where he removes his socks and stretches out on the tangled duvet, arms akimbo. He gropes the floor with one hand, then drapes one of the socks across his eyes to block out the light. His last thought is to wonder what Anna would think if she could see him. Would she be happy? Would she give a damn?

He awakens more than an hour later, disturbed by a dream he can't quite recall. It involved fingers, certainly, stroking the arch of his foot gently, light as a breeze. The sun has moved around and his right leg is now in shade, while his left, with its dark denim, still absorbs the heat. Something is amiss. A sound when there should be none. Has he left the radio on? It sounds like a party—a ceilí, even—in full swing, right in the house, or perhaps the garden. Has Patrick Tuomey walked in with a group of folklorists? He doesn't think so. It's one of those high-spirited parties where people aren't drunk, with music in the background. Music you could dance to, whirl around to. He jumps from the bed and flings the door wide, racing down the hall. He slips back the latch on the half door and listens. But there is no sound beyond chirping sparrows and a lone blackbird on the telegraph pole out on the road. The wind has dropped too.

On the way through the kitchen, all is silent. The light has faded and there are no shadows. He might never have been there before, feels like a first-time visitor, as if intruding. He rips open the back door, his face solemn and puzzled. The night air is dewy and damp, from the lake he hears a curlew's cry. A waking dream, he thinks, returning to the bedroom. Even before he has closed the door, waves of sound return, like a radio being turned up. He leaves the room again. The sound disappears. He re-enters it, and it returns.

He realises he is now out of his mind. Has gone native, or entered some bizarre cultural time-space warp. At the same time, he wouldn't mind being at this party, wherever it is, everybody enjoying themselves and nobody, male or female, trying to leave a marriage or make off with another man's wife. And the music! Wild, it is. It beckons him. Once more to be certain, he opens the bedroom door and places his bare foot in the hallway. Already, the music is dying. He re-enters the room. There it is again, a party in full flow.

He can no longer restrain himself. Now in the centre of the room, arms raised and wide, he takes a step sidewards then back again, holds to the rhythm while staring out the window at the twilit and darkening fort, its dandelions still, bluebells scarcely nodding. He shuts his eyes, follows the elemental fiddles that have played their way into this room, and moves, roused now, with an ease and peace he never knew possible. Here, the hands lightly touching him, guiding him, in a friendly way, pushing at his back, his hips, along his thighs, moving him around the space of the bedroom. Is this the ease and grace which Anna and Henni found after Henni stole Anna? A gift, not one he knew how to invite, now overwhelms him.

Happily he dances, being wanted, ravished perhaps for any and for no reason. He unbuckles his belt, drops his jeans, steps out of his underpants and rips off his t-shirt. He has been included after all, he will foot along through the night, possessed, among the shades of the earth who welcome him with smiles, who dance him, touch him, bring him within. He will weep no more.

9

THE CREATORS

The navette arrives. Its doors slide open quickly and a cheerful female voice announces the Garden Isles Express, stopping at urban stations Paisley, the Trossachs, Loch Lomand and Oban. From within an excited babble of young voices emerges. The transport is fully equipped. There are drinks and snacks, as well as masseuses and therapists. A cabinet of Select Highland Medicines is on display, available to induce a first night of forgetfulness for those who find separation too acute. According to official statistics, none of the Creators has ever come home from working in the Garden Isles addicted to anything except the joy of physical work.

But earlier, there is only realisation. No changing anything. Alistair is aghast. Impossible, that of the thirteen point five million people in Caledonia, Fiona's name should have been randomly selected in that year's toll. *Anyone but us*, is how most people think.

There is no opt-out clause, and when the information appears on their kitchen screen in Block A, her face blanches, while Alistair starts to frantically pick at the dry skin around his right thumb making it bleed.

Everything is understood. But later, his shocked and resentful response is to go shouting his mouth off and get bladdered in the apartment with shot after shot of tequila, so loudly the block HR guy checks in onscreen.

'Everything okay there, Alistair?' the question hovers.

'Aye, just grand!' Alistair strips his teeth in a version of a smile, trying to conceal his tequila tremble.

Somehow he's dodged the cameras while stabbing the sofa with the carving knife, though not audio, the ruckus isn't reported by his neighbours on the same floor, who've been kind. By the end of the long night his trembling hands have steadied sufficiently for him to cope with the ordinary things: walking more steadily, taking a piss and getting it into the toilet bowl and not on the floor, holding an agreeable conversation with a slightly shocked Fiona, who keeps passing him mugs of coffee, which he slurps back even though he hates it.

'Can we deal with this rationally?' she asks sternly when she returns later in the day. He has slept but he is unshaven and in need of a hot shower. Having left work an hour early, still in jodhpurs and boots, she reeks of horseflesh. The location of the Caledonian Stud near Glasgow International is regarded as a pragmatic, if not ideal choice, surrounded by high rise blocks and different levels of flyovers and underpasses for the constantly groaning traffic.

'I know,' he mutters, 'I was fuckin' off me nut.'

'I can do without this kinda shit, Alistair, it's not easy for me either. And you need to hang onto yer job while I'm away! Listen now,' she urges, 'you're a bit too strung out. Calm down or you'll have HR on your case, never mind the school council!'

*

The day after, in the heat of January, Alistair returns to the classroom where he teaches perspiring children about how and why the islands of Mull, Iona and Lewis became Garden Isles. His right thumb is lightly bandaged from the constant nervous picking and ripping of skin during the previous week. His head feels as if specially compressed layers of steel have replaced where his brain should be. But he bears up, carries on. He is a teacher after all, entrusted with the passing on of Whole Truth.

'The old houses were removed,' he tells them, 'including the bothies. There are no more sheep, no more cattle . . . sheep are now bred exclusively in Greenland and Antarctica . . . anyplace else is too warm, apart perhaps from northern Alaska.'

One of the children enquires about camping and the kind of people who once slept in the open, so he takes a moment to digress into the slippery pockets of memory.

'Those people enjoyed open air living, they liked to watch the deer, eagles and otters, aye, folk who would cook sausages over a small camp flame, and rinse their faces in a cold stream. Go to the toilet in the forest.'

The children gape and smirk and he realises that yet again such experiences are beyond them.

He returns to the subject of the Garden Isles, and the dawn of the Hortonomic Drive or—he lowers his voice as if imparting a secret—their country's very own national Garden.

'Everything planted and grown here is for our consumption, for the people of Caledonia,' then with emphasis, 'people like you and me here on the Mainland.'

For homework, they are to begin a project on the Garden Isles. Who lives there, they want to know. Are the people there like prisoners? What is produced and who consumes it? His finger lightly point to holograms of the Garden Isles abundant fields that hover before each child in Eden Primary. *Hold it together,* he coaxes himself, *don't crack here before them.* A chorus of voices rises on the air as the children respond to enhanced colour, rippling crops of barley, wheat, elephant grass and rape-flower. The white wine terraces on the hills of Mull are glossy and dense. The

Creators, all smiling young women, move between the rows of grapes, their hair long and auburn, palest blond or glossy black. Alistair asks the children to observe the machines, which are no longer the earth-bound vehicles of the previous centuries, but hover lightly above the ground. The soil is undamaged by deep tyre-marks, and every last precious millimetre of soil, both Pleistocene and Jurassic, accounted for.

The children's voices curl upwards again at the display of hectares of red roses on the Isle of Lewis, their dewy crisp perfection, then daffodils, and one rolling tract of a couple of hundred acres of aviaries. It always amazes him—heartens him, really—to observe their response to what used to be called beauty. *Beauty.* Within the aviaries, dove breeders are hard at work, handling the St. Columba's birds with ease.

'Because everybody loves St. Columba, don't they? Our own national saint, from Iona!'

The children cheer and stamp the floor until he hushes them. The May Dove Days are better than Midwinter Feasting, because they mean meat and not grains or pulses, flesh and not vegetables.

'And down in Africa, and Australia, and out in Hawaii and Maui, dove is in huge culinary demand.'

Fear and extreme heat created the Garden Isles, he wants to tell them, but dares not. Deprivation too, he wants to add. The nine-year-olds are baffled by the absence of dwelling places in the Garden Isles until Alistair explains that the workers' housing is some three hundred metres underground.

'Do they live in the dark then?' A Cale-Nigerian girl with hair drawn back into two long plaits regards him seriously. But that triggers thoughts of Fiona, spending nights down there after work, possibly for the next two years. He rips the small bandage off his thumb, which is damp and pale although half healed. Again, he struggles for control. 'No, it's not dark down there. Not really.'

The AC system hums quietly but constantly. As usual most of the children sweat, taking regular quick swigs from bottles of water.

'On the contrary, Chidi,' he answers in a contrived, light voice (he marvels at his own acting ability). 'Sunlight is filtered below the ground thanks to a system of fractal mirrors which transfer light to the homes all day long.'

'But my dad says some of the City of Caledonia's people are missing in action,' a bony truculent boy grumbles, arms folded as he watches the teacher.

'Does he now?' Alistair enquires with pleased interest. The question regarding underground prisoners lodges uncomfortably, even as he is trying to formulate answers to the other questions. And as for the prisoners who never quite make it underground, where at least there's some hope of survival, but are kept above . . .

He wants to block out that knowledge too. But they all know what happens to renegades and radicals. He pauses to glance out the window. The searing sun beats down, and in the distance, prisoners from a nearby facility are walked, bare-headed and in hot chains, until they reach the river fence—unavailable for them to slake their thirst.

His gaze returns to the room. He doesn't want to see this. He knows what goes on, and how this group of men and women, parched and gasping, skin raw and blistered, will shuffle, maddened, and then crawl on hands and knees in the sun until their last breath.

He resumes the lesson. 'Caledonia is here, where we live, but we need to have food from somewhere, just like England, and the Republican Federation of Wales and Ireland have retained some land purely for growing things. It was decided long ago to use the islands.'

'I wouldna want t'live there,' the truculent boy with the folded arms announces.

'Well I would,' another boy retorts, pounding the table with his freckled fist.

'Why?' Alistair asks.

'Because—because—'

Alistair knows exactly why the boy wants to live there, and even more why he cannot quite articulate it. With access to his own childhood memories twenty years after the economy failed, and urban myths about famine still being retold, Alistair remembers things before legislation permitted unlimited urban growth. Effortlessly, he still conjures the colours and scents from his Family Archive. There is the Shared Archive, where family memories co-mingle and often create contrary responses within families (because despite sharing, everyone believes their memory is the only correct one), but there is also the Personal Archive, one of the few uncontested areas of experience to which others have no access.

Alistair recalls aspects of his youth that involved travel from one place to another, on foot, for the sole purposes of getting out into the wilderness. That was before what became known as the Fragging—the gradual but violent breaking down of borders within the commercial empire nations so that each ethnicity, each language could retain the autonomy it had struggled for down the centuries. He remembers hearing of true wilderness from his father, he even recalled it himself; fields, hills on which thick purple heather grew though when he was about ten years old it browned and died off, an unpopulated Glencoe where the smell of death from the great massacre of the clans in the seventeenth century had lingered, and bog-land in the Cairngorms where you could see people with tushkars in hand as they cut into a peat bank.

As a teacher of Whole Truth, he is not supposed to elaborate on such knowledge, but despite the risk of monetary sanctions—because class sessions are recorded and banked randomly—he can't resist remembering aloud, so that these children can imagine what it was like.

Patiently, he defines the idea of a field. He speaks of paths and small roadways, of hills and copses, of grass and clover, of buttercups, daisies and wood anemone, of places where sheep and goats grazed. *Meadowland*, he lowers his voice at the word, savouring it. Sacred wilderness, he wants to add, but doesn't. He also describes mountain hikes, but the gradual encroachment of houses, closer and closer to one another as if irresistibly drawn to co-exist like tadpoles in a stream, eliminates the countryside completely.

Some children consider his story of the past to be an invention and most parents do nothing to contradict that view. The parents are preoccupied mainly by childcare, although most don't admit it. But he hears things in whispers and half sentences at the parent-teacher meetings. Women breed and then return to work, with care of the children falling to Sunflower Hubs. Mothers experiencing disruptive and ongoing guilt are entrusted to the Sunflower Therapy unit, which re-trains most of them. They are the ones most likely to confide in him.

For most, the idea of a place in which there is no urban dwelling is inconceivable, and if the wilderness as described by Alistair ever existed, parents tell the children at bedtime, well what poor awkward ill-educated brutes the people were, even if they had all that space to enjoy!

But that afternoon, when the Nursies from each Hub gather their broods and seal them into a navette, Alistair remembers that he never got around to addressing the innocent question regarding the Garden Isles as a place of imprisonment for those who work there. And since Fiona's news the night before, to answer that question might kill him.

The question of who tends the Garden Isle project is vexed, discussed only in whispers, pillow to pillow at night, when Family Discourse Recording is less intense. The Gorbals for example, and the south bank of the Clyde, are peaceful, and the dogs in the streets know that the citizens there can liberally discuss anything they wish under cover of darkness, such is the quality of prevailing law and order.

*

Later, he returns to Fiona. It's their last night. How should they spend it? These precious hours will be gambled moments. You throw the dice and do one thing, he thinks, or you throw it and the result is different. Seated on the tiny balcony which extends the kitchen by two precious square metres, they pick at a final evening meal, tugging at lettuce leaves, twisting morsels of pasta and tomato on forks, both perspiring in an unremitting nocturnal 25 Celsius. Alistair has opened a Devonshire Grand Cru. It cost him a week's salary, but he believes in flinging caution to the wind and is happy to quench his thirst with thrice-recycled water after Fiona's departure. The pineapple and pepper scented Chablis from the vineyards in southern England's own Garden Isles pours with a heavy glubbing into pale blue crystal goblets. They stare into one another's faces, tilt the glasses, then sip.

'When will ye get home leave?'

'Hae'nt a fuckin clue.'

'Don't swear, *a chuisle*. Midwinter? May Dovedays?'

She shakes her head.

'God's sake, afore Oestrus? Before next April?' Bitter anger rising again.

'Haen't a clue, I said. Depends on output. Good fertility stats at the stud farm have to be maintained.'

'Bleddy ridiculous.'

'Could be soon enough though. If I'm a good wee girl,' she almost snarls.

'Aye, do y'think?'

Fiona slumps suddenly. Her elbows are on the table and her head is in her hands, shoulders heaving as she cries silently. What little appetite they had has completely vanished. Even the wine, warming by the second, is wasted. She looks up and scans the surrounding city, where at dusk the lights have come on and the undulating hills of the massive Glencoe tracts are ablaze and twinkling, a rising trail up into a cloud-marbled, mauve and pink sky. How formidable yet mysterious the habitation blocks look in semi-darkness, she thinks, a slow tear making its way from her left eye, down the crevice of nose and cheek, where it hovers above her lip. Automatically, she licks it away.

'So—so I'm to be one a those girls, those fuckin' posing girls—planting and picking for the nation.'

Alistair nods, imagining her face appearing on his school image-bank, of Mull and its gardens. Already he sees her seated on a glossy buckskin, its mane plaited, or galloping across the moors between Tobermory and Dervaig, then coming to a halt to smile out at the world, with the Rock of Columba in the background. Her face, and the faces of the other handsomest Creators, will be broadcast from Argentina to China, from the United Republic of Africa, to the empire of Egypt and the feudal Emirates.

'We won't let it affect us.' She straightens up suddenly and pulls his hand towards her breast.

'Us? Course not, Fiona. What an idea.'

'We're not like the others, are we?'

The words hang. They both know the risks of new bonds formed during the gruelling labour of working in the Garden Isles, bonds which on release are sometimes never severed. Anything could happen.

Later, as she undresses, Fiona stares at herself in the mirror, fingers a piece of her waist-length hair. How often she has literally wrapped it around Alistair's shoulders, warming him, and how often he in turn has nuzzled into the faint musk of it. Naturally auburn and all the more prized, this is what sealed her fate. The hair. The vanity about keeping it long and in a plaited ponytail that swung cheekily from side to side when she walked, but particularly when she jogged. *Yeer a fuckin' fool, Fiona*, she berates herself under her breath. But Alistair will wait and during her contract she'll have time enough to repent the folly of cultivated beauty.

For a while, they lie facing one another, and in the mid-tone hours—it is never truly dark in Caledonia City—they stare again into one another's eyes, as if searching for consoling cyphers for each to decode. But there are no cyphers. Runes. Runes are banned anyway, and divination and magic a crime of obscenity. Signs in the sky. It's not even as if it would be possible for Alistair to go as far as the shoreline of the Garden Isles, to stand and wave at Fiona at some prearranged time as she goes about her day. Mull isn't far from where they live. But the incursion of high walls arbitrarily dividing farmlands and roads, fragmenting lands, splitting orchards, makes communication impossible, as in the old days in Berlin, Northern Ireland, and then later, Israel.

Fiona snuggles against Alistair's chest and belly. She starts to hum, as if to comfort herself. He recognises the air. Nearby an urban fox barks.

> *Thou bonnie wood o'Craigielea,*
> *Thou bonnie wood o'Craigielea,*
> *Near thee I passed life's early day,*
> *And won my Mary's heart in thee!*
>
> *The brume, the brier, the birken bush,*
> *Blume bonnie o'er thy flowery lee,*
> *An a the sweets that ane can wish*
> *Frae Nature's han, are strewed on thee.*

He drowses and listens as she whispers the words. Foxes have thrived. Some people make pets of them and the creatures are domesticated. Alistair and Fiona had planned on getting a fox in the near future, a wily ruddy-coated beauty whose ancestors had once foraged the plains. Eventually, he drifts into sleep, lulled by the warmth of Fiona's body, her throaty song.

In the middle of the night, he stirs suddenly. He urgently wants to have sex. They will regret it, he is sure of that, if they don't do it before she leaves. But again he does nothing except lie rock-still until his erection dies.

He watches her chest rise gently. In sleep, she whimpers and turns away. Then he too sleeps.

They wake early. Fiona stares at the ceiling. Suddenly, she turns towards him and kisses him on the mouth, their tongues are sliding around one another and to his relief, hers speaks to him urgently.

'It's our only chance,' she murmurs, cupping his balls with the palm of her hand. Immediately they tighten.

At first he doesn't understand. In the rush to absorb every last molecule of her, he is distracted as his hands move over her breasts.

'I'm mid-cycle, I'll have you know.'

'Ye said nothing about it last night—'

'I sorta froze. Just couldn't. Too tragic to focus. But listen man, I'm mid-cycle.'

He raises his head and supports himself on one elbow. Then it dawns on him. Obvious. Risky. Liabilities such as pregnant women are immediately dismissed from the Garden Isles, returned to Mainland. But for many it's an obvious ruse and pregnancy has been faked so often that hormone levels are randomly tested. A woman found to be in the very early stages has an immediate termination. Otherwise if a pregnancy has reached the second trimester undetected, in the interests of maintaining good social will the authorities despatch her home, and the pregnancy continues.

'Will ye be able to conceal it long enough for them not to notice?'

But she's too distracted to reply. A sharp intake of breath, she gasps with lust, they tear at one another, and he sees himself falling into her, sliding down and deep into her wetness. Afterwards, slathered in sweat, she turns to him.

'I could be lucky. It's a random check, remember? And I've been researching. Been using progesterone suppressing samples from the mares.'

He swears beneath his breath, but she ignores him.

'A new drug. Nogesterone. The ideal dupe until I'm too far gone for them to be able to do much about it.'

Then, his warning voice. 'You'll be caught.'

She smiles secretively. 'Worth the risk though? There are no body searches. My true hormone levels will be camouflaged.'

'You'll manage to conceal the pill?'

'Right up to the time I pop it straight beneath my tongue.' She winks at him.

'Clever clogs,' Alistair replies thoughtfully.

'We have two more hours before I'm collected. Get on with it, man!'

He rolls towards her, hope and lust surging again, and once more penetrates her. Let him make her brim with possibilities, let his sperm capture her queen of eggs and break it open so that it spreads in a dervish dance throughout the pear of her uterus.

What a frail chance, he thinks later, when they are packed and ready for the day. They stand in the shade awaiting the navette that will bring her to Mull, she and countless other flawless young women and men in summery clothes, sun-hatted and sun-blocked. The global face of Caledonia.

He is depending on Fiona's fertility, his entire life and wellbeing depends on it, to coast them along for months, by which time—if she is pregnant—it will be too late to terminate her.

He has the thumb torn off himself again and the skin below his nail is raw and caked with half-dried blood. *I'm still so fuckin' miserable*, he thinks, *I'm the scabbiest, most desperate bastard in Caledonia today.* But wasn't this what people did when confronted with the intolerable? Oppose? He digs deep to trace a memory back to the previous century, around 2082, when the people surged against the banks, expiating rages that resulted in spilt blood that washed into the gutters of Princes Street, destroying too the floors of Holyrood Chamber.

During the long nights ahead he knows he must believe, as if he had a religion like the people long ago. It used to help some, they were not all like sheep, bleating superstition and prayers in threes below candlelit altars.

Occasionally it helped them to rise up. Be transcendent. Because once Fiona is labouring in the Garden Isles, there will be absolutely no communication between the Creators and their soul-friends on the Mainland. He will never know whether or not she is pregnant, until the moment she might—just might—press her thumbprint to the lock to enter the apartment one evening when he is prepping classes, or even during the night. That would be it, he unlatches the thought and lets it roam freely.

She will find me asleep in bed, awaken me, claim me once more. She will rest her growing belly against me. And I will feel the stir of some wee elbow or knee as the wean turns and Fiona's glorious hair tumbles around my weeping—no—mebbe even my laughing face.

*

As she steps into the navette, they still hold hands.

'Ye'll be alright?' he whispers.

'I will, I have t'be!'

'My woman,' he leans towards her again and presses a kiss to her neck but she bites her lip and pulls away, shaking her head.

Gradually she releases his fingers and half-turns towards him again. Puckers her lips in a playful attempt at an air-kiss. Her smile uncertain. Then she blinks as if blinded by light, but it's just that her eyes are wet. She reminds him of the way some children look on their first day at school. Trying to be brave as they set out. Checking back for the expression on the face of the person they love most in the whole damn world.

10

EDNA

The weather forecast is accurate this time. A cold, damp night, rain gathering force. People jostling to get to their cars or to the tram. Edna emerges from the Abbey Theatre after another play. Annoyed at both the play and the poor performance. Impatient now. All she wants is to get home, have a whiskey, hit the pillow.

From the crowd pouring onto Marlborough Street, a girl darts forward. Between one thing and another, Edna finds a five euro note in her coat pocket. Doesn't care what people do with the money, that's their business. Tells her so too. The girl displaying a sharply jagged split left earlobe. Her ex did that, she says.

Without thinking, she hugs the girl, who looks about the same age as her daughter Flo, currently living in the Middle East. Holding the girl quickly, 'there now, try and find a safe place to sleep tonight.' 'I will Missus,' the girl, not resisting her, irises shrunken to pinpricks.

The girl's earlobe is in flitters. The world is in flitters too. And Edna keeps going. Feeling gratitude, the latest thing people harp on about. The Red Line tram not particularly full, a Monday. Tuning in on a conversation between two youngish women discussing the city's latest experiment in communicating with the world, with New York, where a portal—it sounds very Star Trek-y—at the top of North Earl Street has been set up.

'But it might have to be shut down on account of the carry-on,' one of the women says.

'They should have put it somewhere decent,' her companion responds, 'like the top of Grafton Street or in St Stephen's Green. What are people going to think of us? If it was on the other side of the city, there'd be no carry-on like that.'

Amusing to think of the shock caused by the childish display of body parts. The whole thing will settle down. Surely a bonus to be able to look into a portal and wave to people in New York, and they back.

The tram stops at Jervis and the two women leave, then it pulls on to Four Courts, Smithfield, and Museum. Crossing her legs, gazing out when it stops at Heuston. Cherry trees in full bloom, blushing up through the cold night. How beautiful those trees are, she thinks, as three fleshy Americans step on, bent beneath backpacks. One leaning down to swing her luggage to the ground, the Y of a thong above her jeans, fuzz of dark buttock hair. The tram pulls away, Edna rests her eyes once more on the cherry trees.

When she was a child in the country, there'd been no overweight people in the local town. Only three women, victims of 'glandular'. Glandular, it seemed, was a disease, not their fault that they were large with fat white calves that disappeared down to impossibly small fairy feet. Forgiveness sometimes in that world. Nobody named them, accused them.

Her thoughts shift to the girl outside the theatre. Bony from addiction. Did she have parents?

Edna's parents, fussing and flapping about her wellbeing, perhaps that was because she was all they had, unlike most of the people they knew. Edna's mother owned a string of boutiques around the county, and had decided early on that she might not be able to manage a large family due to a weak heart. Contraception no problem close to the North, she once told Edna frankly.

Years later, and ten years after her husband Charlie's death, Edna still didn't consider herself fully fledged as a city person. She'd settled there for his sake, eagerly learning about his knowledge of antiques, wanting to please and be with him. They'd travelled to Spain with Flo when the child was young. Flo still joked that she was traumatised from early exposure to sanguinary Spanish religious art.

A natural collector, he'd left her with a load of brown furniture and some unsigned oils from the 18th century. She still loved it, cramming the smaller pieces into her now smaller home.

Thoughts like a slow tide. The tram moves on. Just because you live by a little tributary that runs to the Liffey, an end of terrace suburban brick home from the early 20th century, doesn't mean your roots don't run back four or five generations too. Some of her neighbours recall relatives speaking about the Easter Rising, the War of Independence, and the Civil War. Her father-in-law's home was burned out twice by the Tans when he was an infant in County Clare.

They also remember the 1950s and the purple-cloaked demon Archbishop McQuaid, dark prince of the Catholic Church. When she was eighteen, her mother told her that the archbishop disapproved of tampons on the grounds that he believed women might be using them for 'self-pleasure'. At the idea, she almost bursts with laughter but holds it in and instead smirks out the window. The tram is now passing through Fatima then heads for Rialto. What would they think of their elderly only child now, who had made a life for herself in Dublin city, and lives in a suburb full of dog-friendly cafés, nail bars, and young tech sales types out with their French bulldogs every weekend, learning about happiness.

EDNA

She considers happiness something most people had to learn. Only beginning to grasp it again for herself about four years after Charlie's sudden death. Not because he was a bad husband, but because without his unrelenting good humour, though also without his occasional gambling which once almost cost them their old home—the thought of it still makes her break out in a sweat—she had to learn how to go on.

Still missing him though. A razor-sharp scald in her heart. Her daughter had fallen into a serious depression. Thank God Flo met Philip, who had the patience, the imagination, to coax her back to herself. Now emigrated two years. Sizzling in the livid heat of Doha ostensibly to make money for a deposit on a house in Ireland. Flo healthy, working with the audio team for *Al Jazeera*. Edna doesn't worry about her so much. Knowing from their almost daily chats on Facetime, that she is safe. Even happy. And also pregnant. Women friends tell her that you never lose a daughter even after marriage.

At Suir Road she steps off the tram then down the hill in the direction of home. When she was young, and after a few disastrous rentals, she found a damp cottage in Wicklow. Lived there for five years with Guy, a travelling musician from Truro. She travelled daily into the south city hospital where she worked as a physiotherapist, while Guy tried to get his music career off the ground and wrote Cornish lyrics. Then he began to mock her Irish voice even though it was she who was keeping the roof over his impecunious head. In the end, after he threatened her with his shouting, his raised fists, she got him dragged out of the place by the Garda brother of a good friend. Looking back, she regarded him as a dangerous risk successfully avoided.

At the bottom of the hill, she turns right towards the twist of road that leads to her house. The sky has cleared, a quiet chill descends. The moon at its first quarter, pale above the roofs. She draws her woollen wrap closely around the collar of her coat. Cashmere, bought in Capri. It comforts her. The house will be warm. The dog, a short-haired collie called Finn, will greet her as if for the first time even though she's only been gone four hours. In dog time, an eternity.

She slips the door key into the lock, twists. Finn rushes towards her, gives one low bark and twirls around, almost unbalancing from its ebony base a small copy of Donatello's *David* (to her a slightly androgenous study), all smooth flesh, tight boots, a man with his foot on the slain Goliath's hair. Immediately, she takes down the lead which hangs from a brass hook, clips it to his collar, pulls the door behind her again. She heads up the hill in the direction of the Museum of Modern Art, then crosses the road past Kilmainham Gaol, the dog sniffing, cocking his leg at intervals as he absorbs the night. In a comfortable way, she feels ghostly and transparent.

After ten minutes, Finn slows. Time to go back, his eyes signal, and she deposits a black plastic bag of his mess in a nearby bin. Crossing the little bridge over the river that runs beside her terrace. Two lamps on either side of the buttresses throw a yellow pall on the street. She stops suddenly and stares. The front door is ajar. There is no wind. Mustn't have pulled it tightly when she hurried out. Did she hear it click or not? Pausing now before the door, heart thuds—rapid thuds—listening, hearing trained acutely on the interior of the house. How many other women are like her, watchful, feeling very visible after all? Not wanting to become a statistic. Bludgeoned, raped, whatever it is a man wants to do. She holds her position, the door open, but the dog lunges ahead and she releases the lead. She waits.

Then. Knowing by the silence within that all's well, the deep comfortable rhythm of no sound at all, the red lamp in the corner of the hall glowing. Anxiety now. Perhaps she is vague, easily distracted. Forgot to click the door shut. Has to be on her toes about so many things so as not to be caught out.

Imagining it occasionally, how she might behave in 'a situation', as she calls it. Struggle or give in, is that what it would amount to? Stunned by blows to the face or belly? She recalls the words of a soldier who boasted on social media, 'Two to put her down, two to put her out'. Imagining that she might be able to control herself sufficiently to tell the man to hang on a minute, she'd take his penis in her mouth if he wanted, she was old and dry, he wouldn't enjoy anything else. Could she be calm and rational like Emma Thompson in *Good Luck, Leo Grande* who had a list of sexual positions for the young guy she hired? Rational willingness? Or would love itself work on men poisoned with hatred? Could she dare to hug such a man as he ripped through her? She scoffs at the thought, shakes her head.

Then the rage rises up in her during this dark fantasy and she knows that if she was able to grasp a heavy stone, she would smash the rapist's skull.

Unnerved, she bolts the front door, instructs Alexa to play 'Shine On'. She needs something upbeat and the idea of someone's time coming seems somehow right. Yes, *hey-hey,* the idea of the light on a face, shining. She wants to let it shine and shine.

After pouring a whiskey, she undresses. Finn has settled himself at the foot of the huge bed which was hers and Charlie's, front paws sliding between brass rails. She pulls on pyjamas (sea-green, silk, a gift from Flo) and lies down, allows her eyes to rove over the painting a cousin did of the house she grew up in. In the long ago. A deep roof. The arched doorway and pink-painted brickwork. Trees everywhere, the house spreading its skirts on a drumlin rise. The dog, tucked around her feet, sighs with contentment.

She can't sleep yet. Once again risen in her mind, the girl outside the theatre. Hugged her spontaneously. A daft aul one going around like that, is what people would say about her.

Around the house and on the street, quietness. The river below the bedroom window rushes and roils. A mallard quacks two quick watchful notes. She can't stop thinking about that girl.

*

Two months pass. There have been local elections and European elections. This interests her so much she prepares a spreadsheet of the candidates, what they stand for, what their ideology is. On certain days, she feels the city buzzing, making money, full employment again like twenty years ago.

When she leaves the house she sometimes brings Finn on the tram to the city centre. Gradually, she learns where to find people, what to bring. Money, a few sandwiches, cans of beer in her grey rucksack. Not too many because of the weight on her back. Ragged places behind the gleam of wealth: Talbot and North Earl, drifting along Parnell too, penetrating smaller roads off Mountjoy Square. At night, to the banks of the Grand Canal, where the new people shelter, mostly men. Blue tents. Water, beer? No, not social services. Few questions. Their bewilderment. The tents in which they sleep for a night will be removed before ten o'clock in the morning.

Edna doesn't care what people do with the money she offers. They can use it to buy more heroin for all she cares. They're entitled to sit in a squalid patch of ground with the smell of dried piss wafting around them. She carries tampons as well, because young women roam, little scavenging kittiwakes smaller than the big gull men who shoulder everywhere. Sometimes reminding her of the girl she'd encountered at the theatre. They have nothing. They will never have anything, she supposes. But sometimes, when she wraps her arms around, briefest of hugs, quick withdrawal, she senses something shift slightly as she whispers 'You'll be alright, you're doing great . . .'

One morning on Nassau Street, her finger brushes the back of a young fellow's hand as she drops coins into a paper mug. She has left Finn at home for no reason other than wanting to keep both arms free. The boy raises a tow-coloured head, shifts position in front of the hoarding that conceals a new building on the rise. She makes herself squat beside him, her knees stiff. Passers-by, their quick calculating glances. Casually dressed older woman doing her thing for the homeless bewildered. She knows how they think.

'How are you doing?' she asks.

'Not so good, Ma'am.'

Home was Claremorris, he eventually tells her. A row with the old man who can't stand him, so he gets out, doesn't he? Whether this is true or not doesn't matter. All stories are true and untrue simultaneously. The person who tells, gives them the only structure they can at that moment.

'Have you someplace to sleep?'

'Yes, Ma'am. I sleep on Merrion Square, at the front door of the Arts Council.' Now pointing to a sheet of folded cardboard, and a sleeping bag.

She offers coffee from a flask, passes a cardboard mug. Six months in the city, he says after taking a slug. An artist himself. He paints but the old man wanted more help on the farm.

'He keeps llamas as well as the usual.' A glance in Edna's direction, not meeting her eye. His eyes are green, fringed with heavy brown lashes.

'Does he now?'

'They spit if you don't watch em.'

'So I've heard.'

'But it's me head. Dad says it's never been right.'

He likes camping outside the Arts Council because it's peaceful. Big rainbow banner on the railings, cheerful, something to do with Pride and equality he reckons. No smackheads there. He has a small nylon tent for rainy nights. The people there not minding him, stepping over him every morning, or moving around him as they buzz themselves into work. Yeah, it's not too bad and some of the staff even bring him coffee and a bun.

The lunchtime crowd has thickened on the unevenly paved street. Purpose. Goal-ing. Destination-ing. Everybody needed, eyes straight ahead, lanyards a-dangle as they leave desks, rush, rush to fill their mouths for half an hour. Edna is happy not having to be anywhere in particular and in not having confided in Flo about how she spends some of her time. Flo considers herself not judgemental, but all she has is a different spectrum of judgements from those of Edna's generation.

'Do you have a name?' she asks the boy, because that's what he is, a boy of perhaps twenty. 'Fiche bliain ag fás' she recalls the lovely book from her childhood, and the nun who got them to read it. Those sweet first twenty years, all roots and intermeshing of family. In an ideal world. Perhaps the boy's 'fás', his growing, was stymied by his father.

'Mark.'

'Will you stay in the city, Mark?'

He shrugs. 'Maybe.' Another shrug. He stares away and across the road to a crowded bus stop.

'So you prefer it here?'

He shrugs again. 'A bit.'

'How so?'

'Look Ma'am, all the questions!' Words sparking as he settles/unsettles himself again.

'Sorry. I didn't mean any harm.'

'But they're out there.'

'Who?'

'The others. The nut jobs.'

Now she feels foolish. She is foolish, she scolds herself.

'I hope you get to paint again,' she resumes. He grunts and nods as a man drops a coin in his paper mug.

'Still some good ones around,' he says.

'Would you like to paint again?'

He moves his shoulders, rolls them around as if to relieve stiffness. 'If I could get the space. To live. But I can't afford it.' Telling her suddenly, flowingly, about the artists he has seen going into the Arts Council offices. Guys with *huge* canvases. Filled with tortured faces. Abstracts. Black and orange mountains. Blue tree trunks like Hockney.

'You like Hockney?' Edna asks quietly.

'He's so free.'

And wealthy, Edna thinks but does not say. It's time to leave. She tells him this as she stands up, and can she give him a bit of lunch, a ham roll?

He shakes his head by way of refusal. 'I'm alright Ma'am. Thanks for your time.'

Leaning down towards him, bending so that she can place her hands on his shoulders, yes, leaning down to hug, because touch helps, what her mother used to say. Leaning closer to the side of his head, lightly tipping his shoulders with her fine fingers, but he bucks to his knees and pushes her hard in the stomach. 'Don't TOUCH me or I'll fuckin' lamp ye. Don't fuckin' TOUCH me!'

Staggering back, confused. She almost falls to the pavement in an effort to hold her balance, catch her breath. He has winded her. She manages to right herself though not without banging her left knee against the wall—the pain is searing. Surely he's mistaken. His rank smell in her nostrils, stale body, stale crotch, underarms and feet. Surely he doesn't think she's pressing herself too close as if to take some kind of weird advantage? Her head spinning with surprise—no, shock—of it all. Oh. My. God. Has it come to this? Her, practically wearing a Hugs For Free sign on her forehead. And how easily he struck out at her, as if by right. What a laugh! She's pathetic. Blinking rapidly now.

Still shaking but trying not to. She limps towards a coffee shop, The Roasting Place. Calm the nerves. Hold head high. Massage knee. Knocked off her perch. Not so calm as she imagines herself. Okay being an aul one. Not so okay becoming easily rattled. Going dotty in some people's eyes. Shaking, even her thighs are shaking. Not as if the young fellow really hurt her so much as unbalanced her. Lucky she didn't fall. A bad fall signals the beginning of the end.

Not far, two hundred yards or so. Imagining Flo, on hearing about this, which she won't. Flo in the middle of the pregnancy which she, Edna, rejoices in without playing (she hopes) the fussy mother. The Little Family, as she has already begun to call them, will be home for Christmas.

She needs to be more careful. There are all kinds out there, Flo would say. Mentally ill. Sickos. 'God almighty Mammy, would you please not take such risks?' But she will never tell Flo, who might not understand what drives her mother to do this. Who will continue in this way. So much less time, so much to do before she wears her leaf of a life to its final vein. She sips her coffee in the warm breeze, sits outside the café beneath brown and orange striped awnings, staring across at the railings above the College playing fields, her breath steadying.

11

ALL WE CAN DO IS—

The Toporovs had said they would arrive by eight thirty. Jack and Maddie were on the terrace sprawled in wicker loungers. Maddie checked the time on her cell phone. It was now eight forty-five but, she reasoned, this was what holidays were all about. Easy come, easy go. Perhaps the Toporovs had been delayed. Vadim had certainly seemed attached to that phone of his earlier in the day on the beach. Or perhaps, like she and Jack did most afternoons, they'd gone for a lie-down in the cool of the apartment. The special hour, perhaps extended a little, but special nonetheless on account of its careless intimacy.

She ran her eye over Jack, who'd just reached for a G and T, lobbed in a couple of ice cubes, and was now sitting back again. He was golden-skinned after eleven days in the sun and she was enjoying the rested rinsed-out feeling which usually followed their afternoon retreat to the bedroom, like a stillness in her entire body.

All We Can Do Is—

Jack was that rare creature, an actor not resting, who had just completed a six-month run on Broadway, playing Lear's Fool in a contemporary reading of the play. Ben Brantley from *New Village Icon* had raved about it. She enjoyed the contrasts of their working lives. Hers as a theatre nurse in an overcrowded city hospital often pushed her to limits Jack could scarcely imagine, even if he was sympathetic.

This holiday was long overdue. But Maddie returned to her first concern: the Toporovs, who were late.

'Eight fifty,' Jack murmured, squinting into the sinking sun.

As if on cue though, there was a loud buzz from the hallway.

'I'll get it,' Maddie said, swinging her legs down from the little ottoman on which they were resting.

She slipped barefoot across the polished marble floor of the plant-shaded living-room and hallway, and opened the door. There was a flurry of greetings as the four embraced. Jack and Vadim shook hands and slapped one another's backs, while Maddie and Asya kissed cheeks.

'Come in, come in,' Jack welcomed the couple.

'Nice place,' Vadim joked, 'not as nice as ours though!'

They all laughed, because it was identical to the apartment occupied by the Toporovs, except that theirs was three floors higher up, with a complete sea view and no noise, whereas the Davins enjoyed a partial sea view but mostly an outlook on the new part of the town which was still under construction. The apartment was high enough above the street to spare them the worst of the all-night music but once or twice they'd had misgivings about not paying that little bit extra for the sake of total peace and quiet.

Maddie invited the Toporovs onto the terrace. Drinks were poured, ice clinked, and the two couples wished one another good health in their respective languages, *Zazdarovje*, Cheers, and Jack's Irish word, *Sláinte*.

The four had met on the beach. The Russians were sunbathing in full sun at noon, while Maddie and Jack were reading in the shade, both slathered in Australian Desert Factor 60. The man beside them had been in the middle of what sounded like a testy phone conversation which Maddie had tried to follow, wishing she understood Russian. She watched as he waved away two Africans selling shawls and dresses. The men moved along, flip-flops sinking in the hot sand. Others like them trudged the beach daily. She was glad the Russian had dismissed them with the back of his hand. She'd have been embarrassed if they'd had to conduct business with his partner, who was practically naked.

The Russian ranted on. He was certainly laying down the law, and his solid right hand sliced the air as he made his point. In his agitation—Maddie thought he was going to give himself a stroke—the man's phone slipped from his grasp, but she spontaneously reached out and caught it deftly, preventing it from hitting the sand.

'Great save,' he said, in a gravelly voice. 'You play sport, yes? Good coordination.'

'No,' Maddie replied.

It broke the ice. They introduced themselves as Asya and Vadim. The couples chatted for a while about where they came from, Moscow and Dublin, and how long they were staying. They too were staying in the five-star Sol Dorado with its vast golden sun sculpture fixed to the wall of the building.

'Sure, it's probably visible from the moon, like the Great Wall of China,' Jack remarked.

Vadim and Asya found this funny. The encounter didn't have the usual arm's length civil-but-cool holiday vibe. Maddie looked discretely but admiringly at Asya, who was slim and shapely, and wore a silvery thong which exposed the brown cheeks of her slim bottom. She sat casually topless, breasts with dark nipples gleaming with sun-oil as she gesticulated when speaking. In her mid-forties now, Maddie had only recently lost the nerve to go topless, and instead wore a black one-piece. She didn't like Africans selling things to her when her clothes were revealing, not out of prudery, but because she believed they must think Western women were shocking trollops.

As Vadim and Jack chatted, she could see that he was a good deal older than Asya, but with a muscular body and the kind of lines on his face that added to, rather than detracted from, his features.

Asya didn't work outside their apartment in Moscow, she told Maddie as she lit a cigarette. Moscow drove her crazy these days. It was busy, everybody so greedy, rushing here, rushing there, no manners either, no, it suited her to work from home. The conversation between them paused then. Asya read her novel, Vadim texted, his dense fingers stabbing busily at his phone, Jack lay back and dozed, while Maddie resumed her observations of the other couple through her sunglasses.

'Going to keep frying?' Jack teased Vadim an hour later, as he packed up their belongings.

'After our long Russian winter? You bet,' Vadim replied, allowing his legs to go slack at the knees so that the insides of his thighs could catch the sun. He grunted, then adjusted his balls within his shorts.

'Perhaps we meet later?'

Maddie perked up at this.

'For a drink?'

'Drink, meal, whatever,' Asya in a lazy voice.

'Come to our place for a drink beforehand,' Jack had suggested.

On the terrace now, conversation rattled effortlessly between the four. Maddie wondered when had they ever met anyone on their travels who actually wanted to be in their company? People were so self-contained—colour-coordinated beach-combers—and spent their time chatting into cell phones as if they were completely alone. The more stars to an apartment or hotel, the fewer interactions between the people staying there.

Asya was fluent in English, Swedish, and Icelandic. She used to work as a translator, but had given that up and was now working on a novel, she said.

'Interesting,' Jack nodded approvingly. 'And you have time to do it now?'

Asya laughed, revealing a mouthful of super-white veneers. 'Of course. Thanks to my lovely Vadim who supports my project!'

She looked across at him and blinked slowly from beneath heavy eyelashes. Vadim returned an inscrutable look as he sipped his whiskey. Desire? Agreement? Affection? Maddie couldn't tell.

'What do you do, Vadim?' she enquired, because he hadn't actually said.

Now she felt the full force of his pale grey eyes. *Don't look at his crotch, for God's sake don't look at his crotch!* she instructed herself mentally. But the texture of his linen pants was thin and pale and did she imagine it or was he actually wearing no underpants? One downwards flicker of her eyes suggested a dark mass in his groin area, but she rapidly lifted her gaze. Too late, he'd caught her out. *Shit*. She blushed.

He smiled. 'I export goods all over the world.'

'Oh. And what do you export?'

'Chemicals.' Then, in response to her questioning expression, 'Potash and phosphorous mostly. Not very interesting stuff, eh?' He smiled at her again. 'It's not diamonds or valuables, but even so, we are the world's second largest producer of potash.'

Neither Jack nor Maddie knew how to respond to this information although they did exclaim at Vadim's achievement. He went on to quote the zillions of euros worth of fertiliser that Russia exported to Ireland every year.

'I'd no idea,' Maddie said.

'Very big business for you people,' Vadim replied, as if the Irish economy depended on his potash.

'It's a long way from Shakespeare,' Jack said, sounding slightly gauche, shaking his head.

'A very long way,' Vadim went on. 'So when you are being the Fool in New York, you must think of the reason why your country is so green!' And he laughed vigorously. 'Green with Russian potash, ha ha ha ha ha!'

Was he mocking them? Maddie wasn't sure how much he understood about Jack's role as the Fool in Lear, or how crucial it was in that play. She'd have liked him to be impressed.

After an hour, they left the apartment and headed for the restaurant strip. Boats were moored in the harbour, colourful lights festooned along the fake cobbled street, and the stomach-rumbling, almost overwhelming waft of garlic and barbecuing flesh drew them along.

'What do you like to eat?' Asya enquired as they wandered around.

'We're not fussy. Anything really,' Jack replied.

The thronged marina area was criss-crossed by handbag hawkers about to set up stalls on a strip in the shade of the old town wall. Further along, black women plaited bits of coloured thread into the hair of young European girls. Maddie caught snatches of their conversation. She remarked to Vadim that their French was more comprehensible to her than that spoken in France.

'Colony French. Probably from the Gambia,' Vadim remarked with a shrug, wading confidently through the crowds.

Eventually they agreed on an Italian restaurant at the top of a narrow street but with a good view of the harbour. A speeding waiter found them a table right on the street side of a quadrant of tables. Asya wasn't pleased at this. They were too much on the outside, she complained. But Maddie didn't mind. She preferred to have a view of the street and its goings-on. A hedge partition of plastic bougainvillea separated them from the waves of people moving along.

They scanned the menus. Maddie knew without looking that she'd have *gnocchi con gorgonzola* and instead glanced at the wine list. A man hauling a huge bag of handbags and sunglasses paused beside her.

'Lovely designer handbags, Madame?'

She glanced up and shook her head. He shunted on without trying further. Less than a minute later two younger men approached her, offering perfumes, sundresses, and again handbags.

'No thank you,' she said more firmly. Again, they moved on.

Vadim, who was sitting to her left, leaned towards her. 'The whole of Africa is here, Maddie. The whole of Africa is moving, moving, like a swarm of locusts about to bleed us dry.'

Maddie was slow to react, but her facial expression was enough. Vadim looked wryly at Jack. 'You are—as you say in English?—liberal leftie people?'

'I guess we are,' Jack said mildly.

'Some of these people come to Russia,' Asya said. 'They think it's a handy way to get to Europe, you know? But the Russian people don't accept them.'

All We Can Do Is—

'Who? Africans or liberal lefties?' Jack said softly, his sarcasm innocent-sounding.

'Ha ha ha!' Vadim went again, his aggressive laughter filling the air as he turned to Jack and slapped him on the side of shoulder. 'You make a joke of Asya. Ha ha ha!'

Asya was not smiling. Maddie kept her mouth shut. She'd read a report about what life was like in Russia for African migrants.

'Anyway,' Jack made a hand gesture as if waving the discussion off into the stratosphere. 'We're here to enjoy ourselves.'

Vadim agreed. 'It is not for us to resolve these unpleasant things.'

Beneath the table Maddie stroked Jack's leg. She caught his eye and winked, then sat back to listen. Asya didn't say much now. Every so often, she lifted her smartphone and photographed them. As she was on the same side of the table as Jack, she also leaned over close to him.

'Smile, Jack, you're on camera,' she whispered gently.

She arranged her face and smile, one arm draped around Jack's shoulder, the other holding the phone at just the right angle. She scrutinised the picture, then took another. In this one, her head was somewhat closer to Jack's.

'I'll send them to you when I get your number,' Asya assured them. 'A memento of the evening.'

Then Vadim took a selfie, his arm around Maddie.

'You're not smiling Maddie,' he murmured to her left ear, 'you must smile properly.' He waited with the phone held in front of their faces, until she smiled and showed her teeth, which were clenched tightly.

The food and wine arrived, and after a few mouthfuls they all agreed the meal was good. The wine was even better, Maddie thought, happily sinking her second glass. Already, Vadim had ordered another bottle of *Bartolo Mascerello*.

Vadim's phone suddenly carolled out a few bars of *Kalinka*. He glanced at it, frowned, then answered it. There followed a quick-fire volley of a reply and he rang off, then stuffed a forkful of tagliatelle into his mouth. He seemed annoyed about something but by then Jack, Asya and Maddie were embroiled in a discussion on which movies they liked or had seen. Asya and Jack agreed that Lars von Triers' *Melancholia* was really about depression and not about a comet hitting the earth. They both loved it, and also *Antichrist*, which Maddie had thought was revolting and indulgent.

'Who are you talking about?' Vadim interrupted a little gruffly.

'Nobody you would know, my darling,' Asya replied.

'Somebody you intellectuals consider to be a genius?'

'We do consider him to be one, at least Jack and I do,' Asya said with a smile, then reached across the table and stroked Vadim's arm. Her fingers rested there and caressed the dark hair that led towards his wrist.

Vadim, it appeared, was like an unexploded volcano to whom Asya had to make votive offerings. Yet despite his gruffness, Maddie felt more drawn to him than to her. She wondered what the trade-off was for Asya to write novels in that plush Moscow apartment.

As they drank more and more wine, Vadim rumbled on to Maddie. 'So, can you save my life if I end up in your hospital theatre? I take it you know just what to do when I have my first heart attack?'

Asya was eager to hear tales from the surgical front and asked her what it was like to deal with the inside of people's bodies all the time. Did the blood ever bother her?

'I've never been afraid of blood,' Maddie answered. 'It's mostly water, you know.'

'But every day you are exposed to the mess we make of our lives, right inside these bodies?' Asya persisted.

Maddie agreed it was a challenge. Each life saved was a victory. There was no point, she thought, in elaborating on how terrible it was to lose someone on the operating table and how it affected staff.

'So, you are returning to Ireland on what date?' Asya enquired.

'On Friday. Three days' time,' Jack said.

She looked at Vadim, wide-eyed.

'Oh, then perhaps... I am wondering now...' For the first time, Vadim was hesitant.

'This might be serendipitous,' Asya said.

It was like this, Vadim leaned into the centre of the table and confided in them. He had an Irish contact, an agricultural scientist, who had requested a small sample of a new potash product that has just come on stream in Russia. As it happened, Vadim had brought the product with him to the island. 'Only 250 grams,' he said reasonably. It was a tiny packet in a soft padded envelope. They'd left home in an incredible rush and he'd had no time to arrange a courier.

'I was going to post it myself tomorrow.'

Neither Maddie nor Jack spoke. Asya watched them.

'And before I go any further, let me assure you I am not some mad Russian drug dealer trying to make mules of you, my friends,' he said with a grin.

Maddie almost snorted, but suppressed the urge.

'Aha, that's just what you think, am I right?' he said, wagging his finger at her as if she was a naughty child.

Now she felt both embarrassed and annoyed. Was she so transparent?

'So would it be an imposition if I were to ask you to take the little packet in your luggage?' Vadim continued, an imploring expression on his face, then putting both hands together in a praying gesture. 'I can give you my contact's phone number, email, everything,' he added, as if laying all his cards on the table.

Jack looked uncertain, so Maddie thought she'd better speak up before he did his Friendly-Irishman-at-Large thing, willing to please everyone.

'I think you should just follow your original plan, Vadim.'

'Oh, but it's so hard to organise a courier here at short notice,' Asya moaned, her lips pouting softly.

'Well, that's what I think Asya.'

'That's true . . .' Vadim nodded. 'But of course my contact could be at the airport to meet you. You'd have no difficulty at all.'

Jack leaned in close, and put his hand on Vadim's shoulder, emptying his wine glass as he did so. 'It's like this Vadim. We really don't know you. Do we?'

The Russian began to stammer and shrug, looking mildly insulted. Asya sat up like an indignant chicken, her long neck extended and her eyebrows slightly raised at Jack's forthrightness.

'Well no, of course, and we don't really know you, but we trust people, we . . . I thought . . .'

'As Jack just said, you should find a courier here,' Maddie interjected quickly.

The conversation was scuppered and sank. As if to smooth away embarrassment, Jack called to a waiter and was about to order a digestif, but Vadim stopped him. For once, he was not smiling.

'No, my friend, it's getting late. Asya and I will return to our apartment. Any more alcohol . . . you know how it is,' he shrugged.

He waffled on about how they'd enjoyed the evening, thanked them for their company. Asya reached over and told Maddie that they must connect on Facebook. They were both very smooth, Maddie concluded.

'I'm not on Facebook,' she said in a voice that conveyed in its mean tone that even if she were, she would not be friending Asya.

'I am,' said Jack, but he was being mischievous, Maddie knew. She threw him a warning look. 'Sure we'll see you around the beach,' he added lamely.

She was aware of taking part in the most hypocritical of hugs and embraces as Vadim and Asya stood up. Air-kissing and back-slapping and thanks. Vadim dropped fifty euros on the table, their share in the cost of the meal. Jack and Maddie waved after them, then turned to one another.

'So, my friend,' Maddie mimicked Vadim's heavy rolling *r*s.

'A close shave, comrade,' Jack replied.

'Obviously thought we were a right pair of greenhorns.'

'Which we are. Class One eejits.'

'Liberal lefties,' Maddie went on with a snort.

Within minutes, they were laughing uproariously into generous glasses of Cointreau, snorting at their brush with the Potash Mafia. The street sellers continued to pass up, pass down. An older African paused to rearrange the baggage on his shoulders. On impulse, she signalled to him as he was about to pass by. One of his smaller sacks contained fake designer sunglasses. She examined these, then bought three pairs.

They spent the next day sunning themselves, breaking the rhythm only to buy an ice cream from one of the beach bars. As the holiday was almost at an end, they allowed themselves a few hours in open sun, wearing factor 30 suncream, rubbing it carefully into one another's backs and legs. Maddie giggled as Jack slid his fingers to the top of her thigh and in under her one-piece.

'This is the life,' he murmured. It was late afternoon and the sun had lost its intense heat.

'Fancy a swim?' he asked then.

She got up. The Atlantic grew calm at the same time each day on their particular stretch of beach, and instead of great crashers of waves came a slow swell that dropped gently, like an easy breath on the shoreline. As neither were athletic swimmers, this was a favourite time. They would swim far out, then tread water, looking back towards the bleached shoreline at the clusters of sun-worshippers, children darting in the shallows, the strolling elderly women with large abdomens and slim legs.

On the way back in, Maddie hovered in the shallows. This was perfection. It announced itself like a sliver, a sweet awareness, and entered her, a paradisal dart of pleasure.

And then it was gone, her attention caught suddenly by groups of people running towards the far end of the beach. Perhaps someone had drowned. But no. Maddie and Jack came out of the sea and began to walk, then accelerated along the damp sand.

From the water—like sea-spectres—wading straggling people, slipping from an overloaded disintegrating boat. A few women carrying babies staggered through the shallows, rags of garments trailing from their bodies as they held infants clear of the water. The majority though were youngish men, eyes hollow from dehydration. Maddie ran forward as a young fellow collapsed, unable to go further.

'Vous venez d'ou? Vous venez d'ou?' someone was asking urgently.

'Nous venons de Mali, Monsieur,' came the whisper.

She hurried towards one of the women, and took her baby as the woman collapsed lightly on the sand. The child had just died, body still warm, its brown eyes already filming over. Professional habit pushed feeling out of mind.

An appalled silence had fallen, apart from the rhythmic thump of music from the beach bar. Children with snorkels and lilos were being herded from the water by panicking adults.

Other people tried to help, making phone calls, administering first aid. Maddie sat with the woman whose baby had just died. Her face was sweat and salt grimed, her lips grey, eyes vacant. Jack and a couple of Englishmen were dragging people from the water, carrying them to the shelter of umbrellas. Water was being ferried now, litres and litres of it from the beach bar. Finally the music was switched off. All that remained was the sound of voices, frail cries, the silent tide.

She stayed to help the weaker ones onto stretchers, into ambulances, was asked to set up a few drips when the paramedics realised she was medically trained. That part of it came automatically and there was no time to think.

That evening, they moved through the town square again. Maddie had neither showered nor put on makeup, instead pulling one of Jack's shirts over her beach shorts. They passed into a side street. He insisted that a light fish meal and a glass of dry white wine would settle her stomach. She'd thrown up in the beach toilets after the Malians were taken in ambulances. Then she had diarrhoea to compound it, her intestines and stomach gripped by disgust, at themselves as much as anything else.

Now she heard all the English-speaking voices, clusters of people like themselves, mad for sun and hot weather, for a chance to dress up in the evening and feel carefree. She glanced to her left at a familiar Dublin-sounding whoop of agreement about something being 'absolutely fanta-aastic'. Then another voice with greater gravitas joining in encouragingly. Of course. Vadim and Asya. Asya saw her and waved, then said something to Vadim, who fluttered his fingers at them, an ironic smile on his face that briefly dissolved to puzzlement as he took in Maddie's appearance.

She nodded, then turned away. The sight of the dead child, its exhausted mother, had created the strangest reaction, a gnawing savage need to have the one thing neither she nor Jack had ever wanted. To be fruitful and plump and healthy because perhaps this was all any of them could do. Be instinctive. Rich with it. Abundant. She marvelled at the simplicity of it, even if it was too late for them. That was it.

12

I'm So Lucky

Galo and me have made our way home from the town's newest watering hole, the Bogota Bar, which describes itself in the local paper as 'a meeting point for all things Latino—music, dance & the best of vi-vino!'

Someone had hung castanets on the walls, along with pictures of flamenco dancers and posters of bulls. I liked one framed black and white photograph which showed the horses of Argentina being ridden by gauchos with wicked looking little spurs flicked like scorpions' tails at the backs of their boots. But I'm disappointed. I'd expected tangos at the very least, even if Galo and I wouldn't have dared to try and tango. It would have been nice to watch. Instead, it was pretty much the usual pub scene if you forgot the posters. People sat and drank with some flamenco music playing very low in the background.

So we stumble out into the night and head along the canal towpath, taking the shortcut home. There's an unseasonal fog and it's so chilly our breath creates new swirls within the fog and every inhalation is like a ragged drag on the lungs. I've lost my key and we need to get back to the house to find the spare which is kept in the back garden on a narrow ledge beneath the coal bunker lid. This means we have to scale the back wall. Galo shivers and whacks his upper arms as he tries to warm himself in the freezing night. Even the swans are curled up, their heads and necks tucked back in a sinewy letter U that ends just beneath the edge of the wing. He's always complaining about the damp of Ireland. For a man who's survived winters from hell this surprises me. I pause for a moment and tighten the neck scarf on his short Armenian neck.

The back wall is studded with broken glass embedded in concrete but as we make our way along the canal all things seem possible. We've faced down worse than a jagged wall. But Galo is as bad for me as I am for him and sometimes we make unpredictable decisions. We also attract attention in a town where Galo's red jeans and his orange and blue bandanna stand out like bleeding wounds to masculinity. None of the men around here wear colours like that so they have it in for him when I'm not around. I'm his lucky talisman, his girl. I stand between him and all harm as he survives in these backwaters.

We find a bin and Galo hoists me onto it. We're breaking our sides laughing at nothing but trying to stay quiet.

'Shut de fuck up Maree,' he tells me in his heavy accent.

It's amazing how the most un-fluent people can swear fluently in virtually any language, I think, trying not to laugh, but once on the bin I have to get onto that wall. I'm taller than Galo so it's obvious it has to be me, the giraffe with the llama I tell him, both of us with long necks and backs but my legs are longer than his. I glance down at his stolid body, its chaos of hand-scissored steel-grey hair that never lies down even when there's no wind, and I wish he was the one doing the manly thing, trying to scale the wall to see what's possible and what isn't.

It's how he's spent his life, wandering between the possible and the impossible. Back in his own country he got himself raped when he was fifteen, which makes it sound as if it was his fault and it's not what I mean. One night a man he didn't know asked him to carry a load and said he'd pay him. Galo, a village boy, took him at face value, but soon discovered the hard way that the load wasn't cases and bags, it was this big dangling scrotum, and in no time at all he'd thrown Galo's arms behind his back, pushed him over the bonnet of a car inside a rusty open shed and broken him. The muezzin was calling out just then, he told me one night as I held him in my arms, kissing him to calmness on his forehead and temples, and a rooster was asserting itself among a bunch of chickens in a coop, so nobody heard his screams. He needed surgery afterwards. The doctor was not sympathetic and didn't use enough anaesthetic. Galo says the man looked at him as if he'd brought it on himself or had wanted this. It was weeks before he could go to the toilet properly. His parents would look strangely at him, wondering why he was pale, and when he said he was constipated they offered him stewed figs and senna leaf.

Mostly Galo and me hang out because we treasure one another's company. And treasure is the word. There are friends and friends, and on the matter of friendship I've ridden the rainbow of colours. Galo's at the high end, almost beyond colour he's that pure. Let's just say, all things considered it's not every girl he takes to. And I'm so lucky it's me.

So here I am with the triangles of glass glaring at me beneath a street light, like crooked teeth dying to gouge my flesh and I have to lift my bony knee and angle it to find a resting place on the wall so that I don't damage myself. Then I haul Galo up, feeling his wiry wrists. God the strength of him despite his stature. Before long we're both precariously balanced, our knees splayed, arms stretched awkwardly, heads facing one another, and we're like two cats, what with his striped canvas coat and my furry hoodie.

Getting down the other side isn't a problem. There's a bench which the landlady Mrs. O'Loughlin set in concrete at the bottom of the garden many years ago, perhaps when she believed tenants would take an interest and sit out of an evening to admire the view. There isn't a view as such, just the house itself with its white peeling paint, and the neighbours' wandering shrubs from both sides which sidle down into our garden. Neither Galo nor I are interested in planting geraniums and nasturtiums, but we mow the lawn to keep the peace. Mrs. O'Loughlin is uncomfortable with us but can't throw us out as we haven't broken any contract. It took her a while to get the measure of me, her eyes running over me every month when she called for her rent, staring—initially mystified, then later, as if affronted—at my clothes, my hair, my high heeled shoes. I go nowhere without heels which is why they're caked with muck by the time we get home. She's dying to pass some remark every time she sees me, but doesn't dare because she's not one hundred per cent sure of her ground. Even so, she'll shove the rent up first chance she gets.

Tottering around the back garden, I suddenly start to feel sick but manage to control it. I'd love to be able to say it's my time of the month but I can't say that. I mixed grape and grain, that's the problem. Galo steadies me, his arm around my shoulder for a moment. Then we check out the coal bunker, lift the lid carefully, feel around in the dark.

'It's not there,' Galo hisses.

I open my phone and switch it on to throw some light. He's right. There is no spare key. 'Where the fuck is it,' I whisper.

'Relax Maree, we are not thieves,' he says calmly. Then we both stare at the downstairs toilet window. For once, it's closed. Galo normally leaves it wide open, despite my admonishments, but this time it's fixed tight. I glare at him. Now I'm worried about having to spend the night in the open; we'll catch our deaths from the damp air rising from the canal. Already, we're dripping with a mixture of mist and sweat. There's nobody we could ask for shelter, and the neighbours, though civil, ignore us.

'We're going to have to break a window,' I tell him.

'We can't do that,' he says.

I can see the whites of his eyes as he scans the patch of garden with its high walls and impossible catty odours. Seems like every cat in the neighbourhood chooses to mark its territory here. I look up at the sky as I realise the fog has cleared. A wind has blown in from the west. Now there are drifts of coppery clouds and a few tossed stars. Nearby someone's burning coal, the mephitic odour is catching my throat, and someone else has passed by on the other wide of the wall eating chips. I can smell the vinegar and my belly is aroused, imagining a paradisal feast of chips and battered chicken, just the thing for Galo and me if only we could get into the house.

'Nothing for it,' I tell him. 'Use your elbow on one of the small panes.'

'I cannot do that,' he protests, agape, flexing one of his heavily quilted arms as if examining it. He fancies himself in the striped canvas coat and is afraid of ripping the fabric if he elbows the glass.

'We can't use a stone,' I say. 'Too much noise.' He stares at me. 'And I'm not doing it,' I tell him just to clear up any ambiguity.

He sighs and looks at the ground as if considering, then starts to breathe in and out, heavily, like one of those Japanese guys about to smash through twenty layers of concrete with the side of his hand. 'Okay so, here goes,' he says, lunging forward rapidly and bringing his elbow against the glass with a strength that sucks my breath away.

It isn't a clean break so much as a significant crack, enough for us to push and wiggle the glass until finally a large piece comes loose from the putty and falls into my hand. I throw it inside the house, where it drops more or less soundlessly onto the brown carpet of our living-room.

'Hey, we're in,' Galo cheers as he lands neatly on the floor. His automatic fear of authority means he doesn't like to attract attention. Ironic really, given the get up of him. I've tried to take him in hand and occasionally suggest a trip to the better class of charity shop to tone his appearance down a little. How about a simple navy fleece, I suggest, or how about these jeans? But no, he will bargain and haggle in George's Market on trips to Dublin, and comes home with an exotic array of colour and texture that won't work this side of the Bosporus.

Immediately he sets to looking for a strong piece of cardboard to replace the broken glass, emerging from his bedroom a few moments later with something from the bottom of his wardrobe where he hoards everything. His room is tidy compared to mine. The bed is made and there are no clothes lying on the floor. His fur coat is hanging from the door of the wardrobe. Those who can afford it like to wear fur in the Armenian winter, he once informed me, which was why he bought this squirrel coat in a charity shop. He likes the notion of being able to afford his own fur now that he's in Ireland, oblivious to the fact that he's now a marked man locally.

His small plastic holdall is packed and zipped. No reason why it should be, but occasionally he considers moving on, fleeing. I tell him he's in flight from himself but he smiles and says he wouldn't want to leave me behind. Even so the plastic holdall stays. He's like one of those pregnant women who pack a small case, months before they're due to give birth, so as not to be caught out at the last minute. He rarely enters my room, disliking the untidy boutique appearance of it, endless dresses and skirts draped on hangers and often strewn across the unmade bed. I never sleep without having planned my outfit for the next morning, having checked the weather forecast beforehand. He doesn't have to plan his, working in a burger bar. Every evening, he carries the smell of deep frying and garlic and sauces in his hair, on his skin, deep in the fibres of his clothes.

We're hungry. Galo phones up the local pizzeria and orders in. I've put a match to one of those instant fire logs and there's a pleasant glow in the hearth. Later, we'll add the dried-out wood we've been collecting since summer, stacked in the kitchen until needed. I change into a matching green and silver maxi dress and shawl, anything to shed the now filthy jeans, the frilly blouse (which ripped as I was clambering the wall), the fringed suede jacket. Taste counts. Even so, I'm not immune to the sniggers that come after me, or the brazen grins of teenage boys down at the canal lock, the sniggering guff of them, the snide *howya Marees* that come from their mouths.

We enjoy library evenings. The people who attend readings and presentations know to keep their looks to themselves, to concentrate on whatever author has been rolled out for the evening. They are the town's finer spirits, largely female, with a sprinkling of cultured men thrown in to run things. I think writers stabilise Galo and me. In their presence, we can think of higher things. We can make our own minds high like great floating sheets attached with silken cords to our feeble bodies, and consider how lucky we are. Well, I sometimes think I'm lucky, without actually believing in luck. I have a home and I have a companion and I can lead my life as I wish. When we leave the town library, it opens onto a tree-sheltered square. It's safe and quiet, and it doesn't attract the lower elements.

I collect welfare every week, ignoring the talk in the queue, the worst of it unrepeatable even with so-called professional people also queuing, but when I get to the top the woman on the other side is polite and businesslike and often smiles at me. I mean, she really smiles. And that's another reason I think I'm so lucky. There are people like her, gentle islands floating around all the time. It's just a matter of picking up the current that leads you to the right shore.

The doorbell rings and I say I'll get it. I open and the delivery boy looks me up and down before handing over the pizza. But he isn't thinking anything. He's just looking, the way boys do. I pay him and add a tip. He thanks me. 'Thanks Mrs,' he says. *Thanks Mrs!*

'Why do you smile,' Galo enquires as I enter the living-room with two plates in one hand and the pizzas in the other.

'Ah it's nothing,' I tell him. 'I'm in a good mood,' I add. And it's true. Sometimes the booze sends my mood up rather than down. I've sobered up but I'm content in myself.

'What's on Netflix,' Galo asks suddenly, his mouth stuffed with pizza. The smell of cheesy garlic has filled the room and our bellies are tightening too and it's a glorious feast. We drink tumblers of cold water to wash it down, then Galo raids the fridge and finds a slab of salted caramel chocolate, which he breaks up into rectangles and puts on a plate beside us.

'We'll have to get another key,' I say anxiously, dreading another encounter with Mrs. O'Loughlin.

'I'll deal with her,' he says, 'anyone can lose a key'.

'I guess so,' I mutter, but I'm doubtful about how she'll view it. She imagines everyone wants to break into her precious property to squat.

'Once they're in, they can stay for three months and it's legal,' she once told me when she was talking about security and locking windows. 'You can't get them out, it's terrible what happens to decent people like us,' she said, staring at me vehemently as if I was a squatter. But I knew what was on her mind. Why she felt herself victimised in some way. She thought I'd taken advantage. Pulled the wool over her eyes the first dark night she met me when I wanted to view the place.

We settle down and watch *Christmas with the Kranks*. Galo loves that sort of thing. It's only the end of September and the trees are mostly still green but already he's looking forward to an Irish Christmas again. He thinks Jamie Lee

Curtis is hot. 'Yeah well,' I tell him, 'I guess they don't make them like that in Armenia.' I think she's just okay, but then I'm not a man.

When the movie ends Galo is still chortling to himself. It's time for bed, like it's four in the morning and tomorrow is welfare day for me. I can't be late. It's been a while since Galo invited me to his room, but he does it now. I'm not sure I want to go. He can be very equivocal about things. Does he or doesn't he want to do something? And how does he want to? He can't decide, but he always treats me gently, he doesn't lash out like some might do. He can forget about everything that defiled him, because he knows I won't harm him.

I agree to go with him. I undress him slowly, peeling the hoodie that was beneath the canvas jacket, peeling the green sweatshirt beneath that, and the blue vest beneath that again. He's always cold. I've told him he should get his bloods checked but he won't do that. He's afraid of what it might show, although that's neurotic of him. He doesn't want doctors and nurses hovering, taking decisions, referring him God-knows-where. And then I unbuckle his jeans and remove everything else, even yanking his socks off, catching them by the toes.

By now, his nose is moving gently along my collarbone although I'm still fully clothed. He enjoys that part of my anatomy, tells me it's a piece of bone sculpture. He's like an animal on the scent, checking me out. It's familiar, this routine, and I remember the last time, about six weeks before, how long it took him to even remove my top, to allow his eyes to look. There are no scars. My breasts would be the envy of most women.

We always stop right there. He doesn't go below my waist. We move furiously against one another now, and perhaps this friction is as good as it gets, the gripping of one another's thighs, his hoisting me against him, the release of odours as we grow warm, the sweet, refined humanity of it. This satisfies him. I learned quickly to control myself, that it was a small price to pay. Once, when I began to lift my skirt, to draw his hand down, he reeled back. He could not bear the sight of me, my unconcealed delight in him. He did not—at that moment—trust me enough to believe that I want rid of it, that I am his, that a time will come when all things are possible, and he need no longer be afraid when we live together as man and woman.

13

LIFTING SKIN

The day after her arrival, a Dublin family pulled up just when she had settled her things on the pine desk at the open window. Outdoorsy and slim, like people in an advertisement for breakfast cereals or toothpaste, they unstrapped two prawn-like infants from their car seats, then made their noisy way into the yellow-fronted terraced holiday home beside hers.

Although they weren't particularly communicative that suited Dervla, and she waved at them each day as she pulled away in the car, smiling without stopping to chat. Rain or shine she wore soot-black Dior sunglasses that had cost nearly half a month's salary—big square beautiful frames, perfect for Cannes, too glamorous for Carrigbwee. The next-door mother often sat in her sun porch, herself wearing fashion shades, a mobile phone clamped to her ear as the infants played. Her pale blonde, very silky hair slid over both shoulders. Unconsciously Dervla adjusted her own glasses. A public nurse visiting an elderly neighbour back in Dublin had stopped her the previous week right on the street—enquiring in the gentle but not judgemental voice of a caring professional—if everything was all right.

Now, down by the coast, she didn't want to spark misguided interest. She would drive around the cliff road to Neptune Bay, dipping into a tunnelling laneway, down more steeply still to the bluff above the beach. She always pulled the handbrake hard, left the old Ford in reverse gear, but never bothered to lock up.

By the time the third week arrived, her routine was impregnable. Neptune Bay was safe, she thought, slipping down the path. The sand was coarse enough to ensure it would never be popular with the families that clustered on the yellow beach nearer the village, a sandy strip which screamed values, safe swims and loud parental exhortations. Here, bathing was quite unsafe. She could be alone.

She was thankful for the four-month break from the department of Celtic Studies. Not only could she sit it out for these weeks, but with laptop to hand and all her reference books she was making progress on a paper provisionally called *The Celts in the Iberian Peninsula*.

Work on the myths of identity and history seemed a far cry, ironic even, from what was going on beneath her face as it healed from recent cosmetic surgery of the drastic kind—a full yanking up of jawline and sagging cheeks, the removal of bags from beneath frank intelligent eyes, the fine slicing away of the hooded skin above them. To ensure that the banner of beauty could fly once again, she'd even let them raise her brow line. She would return to the academic fold in late September, newly minted—she hoped—with the illusion of youthfulness making her glow. The same, only different.

It was not the kind of topic that got much of an airing in the Common Room where the Marys of her generation sometimes exchanged survival notes. These children of the mid-nineteen-fifties were not all called Mary, but she considered most of them to be Mary-like. Máire from Gweedore, with her long neck, sparkling nervous bright eyes and propensity for travel, had recently adopted a Vietnamese baby girl. It was the talk of the department and discussion behind her back ranged from admiration to one or two traditional comments on how motherhood would clip her wings. Muireann in Folklore was in the middle of a divorce, and Mairín was the mother of four teenagers. They discussed these subjects with one another, carefully and caringly, usually in the absence of their male colleagues.

Dervla had not mentioned the facelift to anybody apart from her husband Dan, who was more equipped than average to deal with anxieties from the secret depths of his wife's nature. Why would she need to do such a thing, he wondered aloud when she told him of her intention, his eyes widening.

'Because,' she replied. 'You think it's silly and pathetic,' she added.

He touched her arm. 'I'm not sitting in judgement. I just don't understand . . .'

For a moment she said nothing. 'Maybe I don't understand either. It's just . . . I don't want to look . . . *old* . . .'

'Well,' he shrugged, 'if it won't turn you into one of those rubber-faced freaks, why not?'

She thought of the many dinner party conversations they had taken part in with their peers, when subjects as diverse as the Booker shortlist, the colonisation of rural Ireland by newly rich city people intent on investment and scenic views, competed occasionally with things of a more trivial nature. Fashion, package holidays on the Costa del Sol, Riverdance, and plastic surgery were understood to be trivial, fair game for a laugh. The latter especially, Dervla knew, disturbed the seedbed yet made some quietly curious. Condemnation all round punctuated with a load of sanctimonious bollocks about how sad it was that people couldn't grow old gracefully. Whatever that meant she mused resentfully. Muireann, mid-divorce and very angry about life's unfairness, had seen a Channel 4 programme about a woman, whose cosmetic surgeon husband had been let loose on her at regular intervals and now had his very own tight-skinned, ever-so-surprised blow-up doll. At this, there was laughter, but also some pitying head-shaking.

'Way to go!' Muireann had said with a defiant giggle.

Eventually, the conversation moved on to a discussion about the Crone in Irish literature, the strength of the Crone and what she represented. Well, what *did* she represent? Dervla wondered about this sceptically, thinking her way out of literature and into the other real world.

It was a two-way mirror, she realised, more and more these days, as she paced the beach at Neptune Bay to stay fit and private. The operation—no, she corrected herself—the procedure had been a doddle. She learned that the language of medicine when applied to female concerns was like a piece of elastic. An abortion was called an 'operation'—this she had gleaned from Máire, who had had one in her twenties—as if to make it seem medically necessary, but a facelift was always called a 'procedure' so as not to put people off by thoughts of surgery.

It had been very straightforward. Local anaesthetic throughout, face numbed as the surgeon marked and outlined, chatting away to the anaesthetist. She had watched him raise his delicate lacerating instruments, and with every fine, painless tug, felt herself being re-created. The youth and radiance still within her, pushed more closely to the surface of not-yet-old skin. She could feel it in her healing epidermis, dancing to get out.

From what she absorbed in her twilit state, both doctors spent as much time as possible down in Schull or putting down anchor in various Aegean ports. As the surgeon gently tugged, or in the case of her eyes, cut and cauterised, she sensed the ease of men at work and at play, and to her surprise she despised them. Mostly though, she despised herself for needing them. She wondered why there were so few female cosmetic surgeons. Did women doctors also pass judgement, preferring to deal with the spectacle of nature in collapse by specialising in other areas?

Another week passed and still she drove to Neptune Bay. Dan was in Kerry, climbing Carrauntoohil. They sent idiotic comically-cryptic texts to one another for their eyes only. Their two daughters were in Mexico learning Spanish. She wondered if they'd notice the difference in her when they returned to UCC in the autumn. She stood in the warm July sun, face slathered in sunblock, watching the horizon through her sunglasses. If she were to sail straight on she would arrive at Finisterre, the end of the earth for the ancients but the start of Galicia in north-western Spain.

She opened her camera and began to move around the pink sandstone cliffs that hulked down the length of the beach. It was, she suspected, a deadly and haunted place and for the first time she shivered. She took a few photos then turned. A seal appeared out in the turquoise sea then disappeared again. She followed its wake, watching until the creature re-emerged. The sea shushed and whispered as it circled and dived. She packed the camera away, then gently patted her tender jawline.

Three weeks after the operation she was starting to resemble her old self. The slightly mashed and swollen bruising had subsided. What remained was a sallowness and residual patches of blood beneath her eyes that had yet to be absorbed. With makeup, camouflage would be possible within the next few days. Satisfied, she turned the key in the ignition and pulled away from the beach.

The cottage was overheated when she got back. She flung the front windows wide and sat down at the table, laptop open. The infants next door were screaming their heads off but the half-written article awaited her attention. She stopped for a moment, listening again. It was the woman's voice, calling out it seemed. She leaned forward slightly and peered sideways out the window. The man was leaving in a great hurry. He stepped into the four by four, shut the door smartly, then snorted off down the village street.

Concentrate, concentrate, she chided herself. She began to tap at the keyboard, and the next sentence came easily.

An urgent rapping at the door disturbed her.

'Fuck,' she said between her teeth, not bothering to lean out the window to see who it was. She strode towards the hall door and pulled it open. The woman from next door practically fell into the hall, bubbles of blood beading a split lower lip. Her mouth opened soundlessly for a moment, revealing blood-vivid teeth. The nose was skewed sideways and also bled. The skin beneath one eye was livid though not broken.

'Sorry to bother you . . . sorry to bother . . .' The thick fluid-choked voice gave out and again she struggled to speak. 'It's the children. Can't leave . . .' Then she screamed, and more metallic-smelling blood ruptured in clots and bubbles from her nose, spraying out onto Dervla's chin and chest.

Dervla could not stop staring, even as she reached for the woman's arm and drew her into the sitting-room. She got the woman to sit down and tried to control her own horror. As she dialled the doctor with one hand, she held on to the woman's arm with the other as if she was a child who might escape her grip. The doctor's number was engaged.

'Tell me your name,' she said quietly, sitting down beside her. She did so gently, as if the slightest movement would topple the other woman into further injury and disarray.

The woman wiped her mouth.

'M-m-*ma*-,' she mumbled.

'What's that?' Dervla asked, leaning close.

The woman drew in a breath and pushed the word out. 'Em-maa... Em-ma... Emma...' she repeated, as if she had just learned who she really was.

Dervla took a tissue from her jeans pocket. It was clean. She reached out as if to dab beneath the woman's nostrils. But she pulled back and mumbled something Dervla couldn't pick up.

'Leave it—it needs to dry up itself,' Emma croaked fiercely and with clarity, giving a slight hiccup, catching her breath.

So this wasn't the first time.

'I'm going to make tea before we go,' she whispered then. 'You're in shock. Sweet tea before you go anywhere, Emma,' she insisted, not sure if she was doing the right thing or not. Emma nodded compliantly, began wiping around her lips with her t-shirt. They were swollen and purple.

'Who did this to you?' Dervla asked softly, two mugs in her hand as she waited for the kettle to boil. The answer was obvious of course and rage rose from her gut so violent she wanted to explode.

Emma said nothing.

'Who did it? Emma? Who?'

For a moment, the other woman struggled to straighten her shoulders, to hold herself erect, as if to say she still had some pride, some coating of protective womanly deception at her disposal. But just as quickly, she slumped forward and gave up. Her body trembled.

'My husband,' she whispered, and began to cry. It wasn't loud crying. It was a miserable, despairing sort of snivel, what should really have been a full-on Medusa-like bellow.

For a moment Dervla said nothing. 'Listen,' she straightened up suddenly, 'are the kids on their own? Oh God this is awful.' She chewed her knuckles. What she wanted to do was put her arms around Emma and just hold her. Maybe rock her as one would an injured child. But she didn't.

'Emma? Are the kids alone now?'

Emma nodded.

'I'd better go to them. Emma?'

The other woman looked up, as if seeing her for the first time. Her eyes now roved Dervla's face.

Again she nodded. 'Yes. Get them please. Bring them to me.'

The kettle was boiling. Dervla leaned down and put her arm around Emma's shoulder as much as she dared. Some of the blood was smeared into her blondeness, around her hairline, running around the edges of her face and down towards her left earlobe.

She hardly knew what to say, yet wanted to say something.

Incredibly, Emma was already pulling herself together, she could feel it, an endurance of some kind. The trembling had stopped, the crying had stopped. Even the blood from her nose was now thickening on her face. Soon it would start to dry.

'Emma, I'm so sorry that this is happening to you . . .' She chided herself for feeling inarticulate, for not knowing either what to do or what to say. Tea. What use was tea?

As she moved to go and collect the children before they drank tea and headed for the doctor's surgery, Emma caught her arm.

'And you? How did that happen?' She pointed to Dervla's face, a puzzled concerned expression in her eyes.

Of course. She wasn't wearing the sunglasses. It was clear what Emma was thinking.

'Oh I'll tell you about that in a minute!' she said lightly, fleeing next door to gather up the babies. They were roaring for their mother.

Frantic now, she entered the porch of the other house, where both infants rolled in a state of ecstatic misery, mouths wide, faces the colour of pink poppies, glittering with snotty fluids from eyes and noses. She wondered what to tell Emma, how to answer her perfectly reasonable question.

If she believed in karma or the cosmos sending little niggling messages, this would be one long memo. It was unfair. One face mashed by a Bad Bastard Husband, another's voluntarily mashed and Good Husband innocently scaling Carrauntoohil, letting her get on with a life that seemed more vapid by the minute.

She would sit it out, learning her own lesson in a way that seemed unnecessary at her age, but sit it out she would, black sunglasses perched on the bridge of her small unbroken nose.

14

Wheelchair Plaza

'You could say I had another life once. No, twice. No, many times. Another life in another place,' Jon announces slowly, as if his tongue was too large for his mouth and he had to decide where to place it before pushing out his words. He sounds hungover except he isn't.

'Where does it all go, and how long does it go on and on and on?' he asks Maud.

'As Camus said,' she drawls laconically, '*c'est l'absurdité de l'existence*'.

'*Mais oui*,' Jon replies in a fake French accent, then breaks up, wheezing with laughter.

'The absurdity of wha? Wha?' he chuckles.

'Life has no meaning,' Maud continues, and bites into her toast. She's hurrying to work.

While she chews her toast she jabs one finger into an eyeshadow palette, then turns to the small mirror propped on the table, closes her left eye and daubs quickly.

'No fuckin' meaning?'

'None. Forget meaning.'

'Well f-fuck that. Explains a lot, doesn't it?' Jon says, leaning over his own toast, raising a mug of tea in his shaky right hand.

They start to laugh at philosophy. They cackle at it, but also at Jon's persistence in asking the question, and Maud because he asks it so often. Jon knows he forgets and that she's replied many times and that's why she's laughing. His tea wobbles as his body convulses, then the liquid spatters in a thin fan across the table.

Later, the minibus collects him. The people in wheelchairs are strapped in, one from Allenwood, another from Derrinturn, three more between Carbury and Knockanally. It's a meandering trip along the edge of the midlands bog before they reach Jon, who is always punctual even if the van isn't. Occasionally there's a delay if one of the passengers refuses to travel that day, or if the driver has to turn back because someone's forgotten to go to the toilet before leaving. Jon waits by the roadside, half a mile from the house. It was his decision to instruct the driver not to come off the main road to collect him, to walk in his lopsided way, twice weekly to meet the van. It's all exercise, he insists, all about getting his life back on track. He throws his right foot unsteadily as if testing the air before he tests the ground. His right arm is stiff but not useless.

He hauls himself into the minibus, then steadies himself. Dario is at the back as usual. Jon joins him, falls heavily into the seat and stammers a greeting.

'Belt,' the driver calls back before he can go any further. Heads turn and half-turn. The people in wheelchairs and the more or less able-bodied, gawking. Up at the front, a woman laughs, her mouth smeared with lipstick. She rocks herself forwards and back, but she isn't laughing at Jon. She's watching the driver, one hand touching her throat as she does so.

'Ah fuck,' Jon whispers, grappling with the seatbelt, drawing it slowly across his body, squinting with his good eye to see where the clasp is. Eventually it clicks home and the driver accelerates.

'Jaysus, ah Jaysus,' Dario says, shaking his head at Jon.

The minibus loops through the countryside on its way to the town. People's heads wobble like tightly held balloons as the vehicle lurches around the depressions on the tarred bog road. They reach Prosperous where someone has put up Christmas lights and a climbing Santa hangs from the chimney although it's still November. There is an extended pause before Jon resumes the conversation.

'I think—I think—Santa is about to t-t-top himself,' he says, pointing shakily out the window.

At this, Dario throws his body forwards, then back again, convulsed with laughter.

'Jon but you're the lad, eh? You're the fuckin' lad!'

Jon feels the warmth from Dario's stocky body as their arms touch through overcoats.

'So how's she cuttin'?' he asks.

'Jaysus, she's cuttin', she's cuttin', an awful state of things. What the world's comin' to?'

Dario's eyes are bulbous, one side of his head misshapen since the operation.

'Isn't she great to put up with you?' Jon teases.

'Who? The missus? Ah Jaysus, she's a saint, a fuckin' saint. . .'

'Ah now Dario, you're not so bad yourself. She's fuckin' lucky to have you.'

'Like fuck she is, like fuck, Jaysus, like fuck.'

A few seats further up, someone lets out a strangled shout. 'Lang-u-agge. Lang-u-agge.'

'Like fuck, ah Jaysus that's awful!' Dario carries on.

Eventually, the minibus rolls down the hill towards the town and joins the stream of morning traffic on the school road. Each time it mounts a ramp, someone moans or shouts an objection, bodies jolting as they crawl along through clusters of brightly-clad children, parents, everybody moving, intent on something.

Then down the main street, past the old abbey, the pharmacy, the butcher and the small supermarket, past the glamour shop at the top end that explodes with finery for women, especially before race week, but is now gearing up for Christmas. Jon sees it all, red dresses and feathery scarves and hats, which remind him of his ex-wife and the hot exciting gaiety of Christmas when they lived abroad. But he pushes that particular jumble of thoughts away.

On the road out to the day centre, they pass a few other clients on the way to occupational therapy.

Jon elbows Dario, who twitches, eyes rolling.

'Another day at Wheelchair Plaza, eh?'

'Jaysus, ah fuck yeah, all on their way. Another day. Wheelchair Plaza? Hah-hah, good one Jon, ya got me there!'

Jon grins. 'I mean, who the hell was John Hogan? Who the fuck was he?'

'I think he performed some fuckin' miracle.'

They both regard the cheerful yellow and red lettering above the wide entrance doors.

'The fuckin' John Hogan-Logan Centre, more like,' Dario mutters.

'Not Logan. Just Hogan. A miracle of some kind. Way back.'

'Ahhhhhhhhh—need a miracle to—set me back on the straight and narrow.'

'In that case then they can keep their straight an' narrow,' Jon says, gripping Dario's hand and squeezing it with his own stronger left hand. 'We're well shot of straight and narrow.'

'No goin' back, is there?'

'Nope.'

A ramp is lowered for the wheelchair users. The driver helps, but keeps the engine running. Towards the rear, another door opens and those who can walk dismount the two steps.

'I wonder what the miracle was, all the same,' Dario says, as he hauls himself forward on the path. Jon stays close. They match one another's wobbling pace. He drags his right leg, lifts it slowly, hesitant before landing squarely on the ground. There's been a light frost, but already the pathways have been salted and gritted. Early morning shoppers are trotting down the far side of the road, muffled in jackets and ankle boots.

'Miracle? Some wanker got his cancer cured. Or a blood disease. There's a big move on to get him made a Blessed.'

'A Blessed?' Dario says wonderingly as the automated doors open and they lead the way into the lobby, a trail of wheelchairs in their wake.

'First step to sainthood.'

'Go on. Ah, go bloody on! John Hogan a fuckin', a fuckin' saint?'

'He has to be a Blessed first, doesn't he?'

'Jaysus. Sure there's no—no—evid-nence, no evid-nence.'

Jon pauses before he replies. He remembers something. 'Yeah, the thing is. The thing is, how long does it go on and on and on?'

'Ah fuck, ah fuck, how long does what go on?'

'It.'

'It?'

'The thing. Life.'

'Ah fuck, jaysus Jon, that's a big question. The biggest, quarest, fuckin' question ever.'

Sometimes, Maud comes to the centre. It's not far from where she works. She can remember things that Jon can't. She can fill in the gaps, some of which are vast. She comes partly to relieve herself from the optimism of her own job. The young brides-to-be, the pleasant grooms, sometimes the parents. Full of it. Wedding-wedding-wedding, a lace-trailing monster, and sometimes she wants to tell the women, including the mothers, to wise up. There's more to life than satin and lace she thinks but dares not say since she's never been married. Instead she smiles and tosses a profusion of auburn hair over one shoulder as she itemises the cost per head for each wedding according to the couple's wealth. That's how she thinks of it, wealth, and not the preferred term 'disposable income'. A morning at the John Hogan Centre is an antidote to flowers, champagne, monkfish and table settings. Jon teases her whenever she appears. He thinks his sister has her eye on the local writer who comes in on Fridays to help out.

'Fancy him, dontcha?'

'I need a younger fella like I need my fingernails pulled out.' Ice-dry to the end.

Sometimes he carries on teasing, but sometimes too he leaves her alone. She needs her own life, he remembers, whenever he can remember which isn't often. Bad enough being stuck living with him at her age even if she says she wouldn't have it any other way. Her own brother? *We're a team. People can like it or hate it. Team.* But she's not here today. It's himself and Dario and perhaps the writer and Sadie the techno woman who shows him every week how to use Facebook. He has thirty-six friends. Some post jokes on his page or click Like whenever he posts a cartoon. But he can't remember from week to week how to log in although Sadie shows him every time.

Today, though, Sadie is working with Dario, with picture cards and a computer screen which offers coloured boxes for Dario to click on depending on his response to the images. Jon is paired up with the writer, a gangling man called Brian with a clipped little trowel of a beard. Brian wants Jon to tell a story. It can be about anything. It can be memoir, Brian says, if Jon wants to speak about his own life. Or it can be a short story if he wants to invent it.

Jon gives a long wheezy laugh. 'Ah fuck, you couldn't make it up.'

'How so?' Brian asks.

'Isn't life—' Jon hesitates as he tries to organise the phrase in his head before he speaks. 'Isn't life—stranger than fiction?'

Brian nods and smiles.

'And my life is a fuckin' disaster. At least, since the accident it's a fuckin' disaster. Like something a writer would make up—except that it's true.'

On the other side of the room Dario lets out a whoop at something Sadie has just said, and a stream of *fuck-fuck-jaysus-fuck-fuck* briefly stalls several other conversations. Jon shakes his head at Brian. 'He's d-disinhibited. Like me, only w-w-worse.'

Brian slides a sheet of A4 across the table, then asks him to stop and think.

'About what?'

'You.'

'Where will I begin?'

'Wherever you want.'

'Ah fuck. Don't come on like one of those w-wanker psychologists in the hospital. I can't lead the discussion. I forget.'

Jon has begun to shake his head agitatedly. He raises his left hand and holds it across both eyes as if to push the frustration that leaks out of him back into his head.

Fifteen minutes later he clasps a mug of strong black coffee with both hands. There are a few scrawls on a page. The words *Hong Kong*, and *the kids*, underlined by a pink marker.

'I remember a lot,' Jon says, looking at Brian with his good eye, indulging him.

Brian waits while Jon considers.

'We were on top of the world . . . back then. Her and me.'

Morning at the centre has taken off. Some men and women play card games, others work at laptops. Yet others are poring over a newspaper. A woman in a motorised wheelchair buzzes herself around the room, body rigid, her mouth pulled slightly down on one side. A thin track of saliva runs towards her chin. She stops beside certain groups.

'It's always another day,' Jon observes drily. 'Always another fuckin' day.'

Back in Hong Kong, it was always another day too. Another day to work, to play, to shop, to eat, to bring the children to the beach at the weekend. Each day unfolded like a giant warm leaf from an incessantly growing tree in which they were allowed to live and thrive. It was so different from Ireland. Money was flowing, they could do what they wanted. How he basked in their life. These memories are coming to him, but he can't write them. The words are jumbled.

'F—ffff-uck!—if I could paint it—photograph it—that'd be easier. I can't string the thing together, but I see pictures. Every frame—of that time—every fuckin' frame when we were—like *magic* together. Christ! I have to get my life back on track . . .'

Brian leans in, places his hand lightly on Jon's arm. 'Do you have a few pics from that time?'

'Some.'

'Bring them in next week. We can talk about them.'

Jon turns and stares hard at Brian, as if seeing him for the first time, his good eye boring straight into Brian's head while the one with the blown pupil stares off to the left.

'I'll consider that,' Jon finally answers—suddenly, briefly—a negotiator again. 'I'll consider it and r-revert back to you.'

Brian pushes Jon's diary towards him. 'Make a note,' he instructs.

'Oh. A minor detail that,' Jon laughs, picking up pen and bringing left hand slowly down towards the open diary page. He pauses, looks at Brian. 'Eh, I've forgotten. What am I reminding myself to d-d-do?'

'To bring in a few Hong Kong photos next Wednesday.'

Brian watches as Jon writes. It's more than a scrawl. It is legible and careful. It is a complete correctly spelled sentence, with i's dotted and t's crossed, things carried from childhood, not erased despite the bloody broth of his injury.

But the moment he writes the note to himself in the diary, images buzz through him, like bees dripping honey of the past. Haltingly, he talks. There's the journey to the East, the huge apartment the company found for him, Ireland's top man. 'Our Man in Hong Kong,' Maud used to call him. The parents bursting with pride. The deal. Selling Ireland to the Chinese. He had the pitch, the attitude, the brains.

'That was the time the Taoiseach came—a real Taoiseach—'

He tells of the boost the visit gave to them in the office. 'The Chinese were hard bargainers, feng shui or no fuckin' feng shui. The s-superstition of them—they'd chop their own mothers' heads off rather than miss closing a deal—anything—right c-cunts some of them. But I liked them and they liked me.'

That was business. But there was something else. Her. Their life. One child already born before they left Ireland. Then two more—blond rapscallions of children with very blue eyes, jewel eyes that had the Chinese women swarming around them. The women would poke the kids, examine their skin, feel their fine curly hair, peer at their eyes until he had to intervene.

'Rapscallions, Jon?'

'I didn't lose everything, you know, Brian. My—my fuckin' vocabulary—remains, er—v-voluminous, you might say—if anything, it's fuckin' improved!' He explodes with laughter at his own joke.

He could do the *Irish Times* crossword. Sometimes even Maud couldn't answer the clues, but mostly, he could. He would hold one hand over his right eye and squint at the print, then painstakingly, with shaking hand, inscribe the answers.

There had been parties. Always parties. And Isobel, or Izzy, as he'd called her, was a Main Attraction.

'You know what a Main Attraction is, I take it?' he looks sharply at Brian, who nods.

Such a good time they'd had, the children's *amah* available to babysit as they headed out to the ex-pat gatherings. He'd bought Izzy a three carat diamond ring. But she'd lost it. Always a bit scatty, that was Izzy. He bought a replacement on a day trip to Kowloon. The jeweller assured them of the investment they were making. Like fuck.

There was one couple they were very friendly with. The neurologist and his dentist wife. Izzy liked them.

She'd go on shopping sprees with the wife, then they'd party together at weekends. Izzy was good company, ready to join in, learn new things in a new culture. Jon knew the neurologist had noticed her, by the way he never called her Izzy, but Isobel. He pronounced the name carefully, plummily, in his enunciated English accent.

'Are you with me?' he demands of Brian.

'It must have been a shocking contrast to come home. Why did you come home, Jon?'

At this, Jon's face darkens. He inhales deeply and puts his left hand on one knee, leaning forward stiffly as if in pain. His head is shaking as if to say no to something.

'Vanity.'

'How so?'

'The p-prospect of heading up my own factory.'

'Surely you mean ambition?'

'Look where it fuckin' got me.'

'What was the factory producing?'

'Surgical gloves, c-c-condoms. Of course, back then in—in—the Republic of Coitus-fuckin'-Interruptus, the condoms were for export.'

This time, he doesn't laugh. His thoughts go off the Richter scale of memories true and false. A hurled montage, incomprehensible because he can't complete the picture. As he tells it, some memories are in the wrong place or on the wrong timeline. There was one trip on the

Trans-Siberian Railway. But there was also a trip down to Australia, and was the neurologist with them or not? He thinks so. He remembers their group diving boozily off a boat outside Brisbane, and jokes about man-eating sharks. Then the incredible turquoise of the water, the blue groper fish, and other fish with fancy fins and tails. Izzy was like one of those. Her blue and pink bikini, little sequins along the straps sewn by busy Chinese hands. A beach barbecue later. He was drunk but he wasn't blind. The pair of them. Flirting. Pacific sunset. Sea salt on his lips.

Then. One winter's morning back home. An early start for the fifty-mile drive to the factory. Straight across the frosted road and into a tree. Despite the fancy car the company had outfitted him with. Six weeks later, he woke up naked and in a wheelchair. The nurses showered him with cold water which catapulted him back to life in an indignant stream of invective, his new working vocabulary.

Later, Izzy called him a useless fucking vegetable who forgot to insure his own life and had left them penniless. She'd never signed up for this, she told him. Now she had to go out and work for a living to keep a roof over their heads. She told him she hated him.

'The thing is—the thing is—' he speaks very slowly to Brian. 'I keep seeing these—these pictures—like, there's something I was beginning to know, when we were in

Hong Kong. My—fuckin'—intuition? That neurologist. Maud has a good pair of secateurs for the garden. If I could bloody send her to find that b-bollocks—'

Despite himself, Brian smiles. 'What we can do is write out the bones. The bare facts. About Hong Kong, I mean. Talk about your job and about some of the people you met.'

'Not my ex-wife.'

'Not your ex.'

On the journey home in the minibus, a melting exhausted silence. The passengers are too wrung out to shout or talk. Dario swears even more now that he's tired because the ordinary words have gone into hiding in his mashed brain. Some of them will return tomorrow. But first his wife will give him his dinner and settle him in front of the television, then later she will help him to bed and he will rest, close his mouth, his bulbous eyes, be silent.

'Ah jaysus, Jon, jaysus! What a day, eh? What a fuckin'—a fuckin' busy day that was, eh?'

'Yeah,' Jon grunts.

Maud meets him at the end of the road in her car.

'I'm out tonight,' she tells him as he lowers himself into the passenger seat. She puts the car into first gear and pulls onto the road.

'You've got a—a date?'

'Nothing special. Just going to the Indian.'

When they get into the house she goes upstairs. Jon hears the thrumming of the shower, music on the radio, her busy footsteps. Maud has a life, he thinks. It's on track. An hour later, she comes down in a blue dress with a short leather jacket over it. She's wearing new long boots, and her cheeks shimmer with some of the gunk she's applied. But he's absorbed with the crossword.

'Help me with this f-fuckin' clue. Please,' he mutters, putting down the pen and crossing his arms awkwardly.

'Read it out.'

'*Sick-feeling-for-the-French-writer.* Six letters.'

Maud pauses to think. Then she smiles.

'Come on. You know this one.'

'I fuckin' don't. Sick feeling and a fuckin' French writer?'

'You know the writer.'

'Do I?'

'Think.'

'Wha? Wha—for fuck's sake.'

'We mentioned him this morning.'

'We did?'

'The meaning of life fellow.'

'Who da fuck is that?'

For once, she sighs. 'Albert Camus. We were talking about him at breakfast. Have you forgotten?'

But that conversation had slipped into the sunken ship in his brain, where everything floats. The things he can intuit are also down there, like corpses. He can't put the shape of fact on them, or haul them up to the surface like a gleaming dancing net full of live fish.

'Bollix that I am. All gone. Can't remember.'

Well it's not Camus. It's the other one.

'Maybe not everything is worth remembering.'

Jon is frustrated. Some things are worth remembering. He looks up from the armchair, as if the answer is written on her face.

'The answer is *nausea*,' she says.

'Nausea?'

'One of Sartre's novels.'

'Ahh, I wouldn't have known that. Even years ago.'

He looks puzzled, and calls her back just as she is about to go out the door.

'So where does it all go away, and how long does it go on and on and on?' he asks.

She smiles. 'As Camus says, *c'est l'absurdité de l'existence.*'

She winks at him and suddenly they're both breaking their sides. Tears are running down his cheeks, his face is red at the idea of it.

'*Ah, oui, oui!* Now get outta here,' and his gargle of laughter fills the room even after she's vanished and the front door has slammed.

15

COINS FOR THE FERRYMAN

The dog found the body. It was a male with a fractured skull. They were near the riverbank on the far side of the arched bridge where the current flowed smoothly. Upstream, a weir, where a heron would wait on a rock in the silver-grey cascade. Laura had made her way all summer along the broken track on the quiet side of the bridge, past companionable trees, to have breakfast. At that point the ground flattened, held firm by soft grit at the water's edge. She would perch on a collapsible stool and unwrap her yellow neck-scarf, slugging coffee poured flask to red tin mug, pulling at hunks of buttered sourdough as she stared out at the river. Afterwards, she would unpeel two small oranges.

She might or might not alert the police. It was her discovery. The dog was not going to get the credit. He'd halted, sniffed, then ripped ahead through the underbrush. She thought he might have found a hedgehog or dead squirrel, his tail wagging at the delight of a flesh find.

She'd often wondered who came at night. Some mornings the evidence lay scattered—crisp bags, chocolate wrappers, empty beer cans, a condom, and lately the occasional face mask—but she'd never felt afraid of coming alone and would pass by the detritus and move towards the water's edge. A woman can decide to be afraid and curtail her movement. Or she can carry on as if she owns the space of the world along with all the other people: the men, rich women, people with jobs. She has a job to do but it isn't a paid one.

Already clusters of flies and preoccupied ants feasted on the stilled and darkened cranial outpouring. She observed a large damselfly hovering over the head before it passed on about its business towards the shallows. She was relieved not to see actual brain matter, remembering an unsettling image from the movie *Pulp Fiction* involving a clotty eruption of shot meninges in the interior of a car.

She leaned over and examined the white open-eyed face. Middle-aged. Pale skin with few lines, beardless, the eyebrows a mouse-fur colour. He wore cream corduroy jeans, now grass stained and muddy on both knees, and above that a jacket of brown and white striped seersucker. In the course of the attack one shoulder had been ripped loose and the fabric and some padded filler hung forlornly in the grass. Beneath the jacket a white t-shirt carried spatters of blood. It could have been a fancy art pattern, she thought, except it wasn't. Out of instinct she said a prayer for him in her own words. Her boot toed the left leg, which lay spreadeagled from the groin. The body wasn't far from the water, in fact the right hand fondled the river which trickled and curled through remarkably clean fingers. Not flat-topped digits, but long and tapered, with clean trimmed nails. He lay in rigor mortis, which meant death had occurred recently. After twelve hours, the body would move to its next phase and soften.

There was nothing to be done. Not for her the flight up the river path to the road, head to phone, screaming for the police, or pointing to random passers-by about a body, creating a respectable melodrama for them to feast on in the village like the flies already soaking up the man's coagulating blood. *Shocking really . . . this is a quiet place,* she imagined someone telling a news reporter, or . . . *we won the Tidy Towns last year . . . we all know one another here . . .*

She hitched her belongings further along the bank, away from the body, and set down the stool. Already, the dog had lost interest in the man and would now stick close, awaiting his daily crust of sourdough as well as the drop of coffee after she'd drained her mug. Although the vet scolded her about stained teeth, the dog loved his coffee. She wouldn't deny him.

Mornings were usually sunny and the usual summer deluge rarely poured before eleven o'clock. It suited her not to go to her mother Grace's house until after eleven, gave her time to build herself up. Preparation was essential. Breakfast in the peace and quiet. Difficult to get Grace to leave her bed. If she insisted on remaining there so much, Laura would sometimes rant, they'd have to get a hoist, and how would she like that?

But it all went over Grace's head. The big press off the kitchen which used to hold Lukas' giant containers of oatmeal, dried pulses, and raisins was now stacked with tight bundles of incontinence wear with special ties and adhesive tapes, a supply replenished by the local health office as soon as it threatened to run out. Nobody ever considered the hazard to the environment presented by elder care, Laura sometimes reflected. All those plastic aprons, gloves and never-ending nappies? It wasn't solely the genuinely infantile whose needs created excess but the senile infantile, liquids and emanations comparatively vast and all with a right to life until they decided to let go of it. Unlike the poor sod she'd just discovered. *He* didn't have any choice in the matter, she mused.

Occasionally, while counting out her mother's morning tablets, Laura considered the medical armaments prescribed by the hospital doctor after Grace had fallen down the stairs and had to be hospitalised. She considered all that kept the old heart beating, blood pressure low, circulation pumping. But none of these tablets would ever help her to walk again, to wash herself, dress herself, hold a knife and fork, and none would restore her memory. So a few weeks earlier, Laura had stopped dispensing the night-time blood thinning tablet. She felt certain that there were other caring daughters and sons throughout the land who attempted to accelerate the natural process, whether from kindness or self-preservation.

Just as the sequence of time in terms of actual hours and minutes regarding the reporting of a dead body seemed to her not urgent, so too she considered the sequence of memory. In dementia, past, present and future were moveable feasts to enter at will and in any order. Her mother remembered all far past events in exact detail, and songs she had learned in Irish and English as a young woman. She could even call up some school German and would sometimes greet Laura by chanting out the days of the week, except that she had been taught to say *Sonnabend* for Saturday and not *Samstag* as Laura had been later taught in the same school. She liked to hear her read Yeats's *The Lake Isle of Innisfree* and also Padraic Colum's *An Old Woman of the Roads*. The images of speckled delph in that poem, and of piled-up turf against a cottage wall, appealed to Grace who pitied the homeless old woman.

Upbeat weekly emails landed from Laura's brother in Australia and her sister in France. Travel was now difficult even if they wanted to come. They were all soft talk and horse-shite as far as she was concerned, waving and laughing on Skype calls to Grace, displaying the latest celebrated grandchild from a patio in Perth or a geranium-packed atelier outside Lyons. Blind in one eye, her mother could hardly see them on the laptop screen and although she smiled and nodded as old people were supposed to, grandchildren no longer interested her. At such moments Laura's sadness deepened, mostly because of their assumptions about what might interest Grace. Laura had often imagined her mother's thoughts of the past like a stream of crossing currents and oppositional pulses of memory. Such busy traffic left little room for the present.

Breakfast by the river was one way of lightening the burden which sometimes built within her, a bit like the thick river flow before it hit the weir and poured over in a ferocity of grey and white around the reed-thin legs of the watchful heron. She would leave her bed in the house she shared with Lukas and head off. It had taken them four years to build a wood and glass basic eco-home with a few airy high-ceilinged rooms, finally completing two guest bedrooms last year. Now all that remained was to make a garden, with rainbow pots, creamy gravel and no mowing. Lukas wasn't the most energetic of men, but neither was she the most energetic of women, except where caring for Grace was concerned. And Lukas often helped because she could not physically lift her mother. He would get the old woman up, changed, dressed, and down to the table for her dinner in the evening, before helping her into the sitting-room where she would stare at the television for a few hours, channel-hopping to find the noisier game shows.

She poured herself a second mug of coffee, now settled comfortably on her stool. Here by the river something happened even when nothing happened. Her life melded into something utterly contained and safe, yet extraordinary. In recent years she'd wondered if she was experiencing synaesthesia, because sometimes she could perceive every invisible but active cell around her as a very physical throb within her brain. She also imagined she could feel the Fibonacci sequence of young ferns on the brink of unfurling, except right in her brain as if it were being gently tickled and stroked to awareness. Here all edges and anxiety vanished, were part of some process that was almost acceptable to her. Her mother's decline was inevitable and because she, Laura, wanted to get on with grief and the rest of her life, she urged on the future.

How often had she tiptoed into the still morning bedroom, hoping—yearning—that her mother would have died in her sleep? But no. The broad chest rose and fell gently as she dozed.

'Enjoy her, she won't always be there,' someone once remarked. She managed to nod in agreement with the empathetic-as-a-stale-fish friend. Ever since, if anyone asked after Grace she told them nothing beyond a basic *she's-doing-very-well-thanks* and promptly changed the subject. None of *them* had had to lie awake in a fret about the women who came in twice daily from the so-called caring organisation but who forgot to do basic things such as empty the bins which were crammed with her mother's used personal care items, or run the dishwasher, or encourage her mother to get up. The caring organisations really amused her with their sanctimonious advertisements on television portraying a facially erased old person nodding gratefully, and some young one with eyebrows like a character from Peking Opera in the Qing dynasty peering down into their face. It fucking sickened her.

So, a little tweak here or there. In time the lack of a blood thinner would do its work. She was relying on that, she told Lukas.

She watched the dog for a few moments as he entered the river shallows, paused, then lapped at the water. Above clouds were gathering. It wouldn't be long before it rained. She gathered up her mug, flask and plate, shoved them into a canvas shoulder bag, folded the stool and clicked her tongue to call the dog to heel.

There was one more thing to do before the village began its speculations. The discovery would make national news. How wonderful it would be, if delusional also, to live in a place where murder was never really reported. She knew from listening to a forensic scientist on a podcast that Irish people excelled at disposing of dead bodies. And although she doubted this information, apparently they didn't just run away and forget about it, they worked hard to delay and conceal. They burned the body, or dismembered it, or buried it first, to delay things. Or, as in her case now, they failed to report. Or they withheld pills and hoped for the best.

She closed in on the body again and watched. He had probably been a sweet child who went to school with other boys, came home, enjoyed his dinner and told his Mammy what had happened that day and what the teacher had said. She prodded the torso with the edge of her boot. Still in rigor mortis. She searched the pocket of her jacket, found the spare coins she always kept for when she visited the city, to give to homeless people on the streets. She withdrew a two euro coin and a fifty cent piece, turned them over thoughtfully between thumb and forefinger. Quickly, she spat on each coin and rubbed it clean with her yellow linen scarf. Then having second thoughts, she turned to the river and rinsed the metal pieces again, feeling water flow like a balm through her fingertips. How fresh it was, how sweet and free, she thought, suddenly wanting to remove her clothing and swim there. Again, she dried each coin carefully.

There was surely enough there for a crossing, she thought, then chided herself momentarily for such a fanciful notion as thinking of Charon, the Greek ferryman who transported the dead across the river Acheron. She approached the body and squatted. Flies rose in a fizz. The natural process was well underway. But the ferryman would be content. Even with the head turned to one side, both coins remained in position, making black skull-holes of the face, closing off the poor shocked eyes from the light.

She stood again, then walked away, the dog trotting ahead of her. When all the fuss died down, she would return, but with Lukas, to swim in the morning light.

16

Walking Ghosts

In February, Jane's mother died. That spring, the tantalising expectation of land coming on the market, like the unignorable reek of sprayed manure, rose in the air above the fields, twisted its way through the hedges, beneath the branches and entered the nostrils of several farmers.

Once David Kelly got wind of Maggie Mooney's death, he wasted no time in offering to come down from Tyrone. It was too soon, Jane said on the phone in April. Her mother was hardly buried. She hadn't made up her mind about what to do. Perhaps in the autumn, he could call again.

She was in no hurry. She could do as she wished with the small farm of sweet green fields with road frontage on both sides of the hill it spread across. There was even a lake, with fishing rights. Years before, Jane had planned on building a wood-clad house with two huge bedrooms, an open plan layout downstairs and a separate room for her architectural practice, in a high corner of the lake field with the choicest view of the lake itself. There would be geothermal heating, solar power, and to hell with the cost. She would move back to her home county, settle in, design for a new clientele near the border, and watch sunsets till she dropped.

But the reality of Maggie's death changed her thinking over the summer as she packed up the old house, as her heart creaked and flaked with absence. Thoughts of her silver-haired mother churned constantly in her brain. She had lain in the downstairs sitting-room for three months before the end, a small patient form awaiting release, stiffening, her voice weakening, although there was nothing in particular wrong with her apart from the arrival of death. There was also the material loss of things she now had no room for. Attachments, even if useless. She learned more about people's tastes. How nobody wanted brown furniture or beautiful old china, nor did they have any appetite for chased silver. Maggie's dark and gleaming mink coat had gone to one of her carers who liked such things, even if it would never fit her and would probably be sold. Everything came down to bucks and advantage.

At work, she designed houses. If people were happy then her job was done. Clients wanted sun-and-light attracting shapes as extensions so that they could bring the garden in, whatever that actually meant. They wanted modern leathers and marble and granite and polished concrete, they wanted brushed brass taps and Belfast sinks. She watched as several of her mother's Edwardian dressing tables and wardrobes entered the skip at the back of the house. Some pieces she gave away to younger people who would upcycle them, which meant eau-de-nil paint and then a bit of sanding to make them look worn and antique although they already were feckin antique.

The place sold quickly apart from the other farm, which was on the other side of the road and a separate matter. In no time, the new couple informed her they'd be demolishing the house. What they were on the brink of building wasn't so different from what she favoured in her practice in Drogheda. High contemporary. White. Black. Grey. Elements of rusted cladding as a feature down the west elevation. She suppressed an ironic smile when the new owner informed her that she'd be ordering a pair of peacocks, that it would be lovely to have them around the place in such a mature garden. She wondered what she would think when they began shitting everywhere, which they would, squawking around the place night and day.

The land was another matter. David Kelly, true to his word, phoned again in September. One Friday they met in the café of a general hardware store. It was full of timber-faced women leaning in closely together, some of them masked, others not. The noise of the coffee machine was deafening, but the Greek salad she stuffed into herself reminded her of the last holiday she'd spent with Maggie, in Rhodes. That was before travelling with her mother would have required an army of helpers, before it all became too much for Jane, who used to travel with tranquillisers in her bag.

Kelly had it in mind to join her land up with his other holding, recently purchased after the farmer McGrory died, leaving a bungalow with a view of the same lake Jane's adjacent land overlooked. He had ready money, he told her.

'I can pay you fifteen smackeroos, no bother, no bother at all to start with.'

She said nothing, conscious of eyes here and there flickering in their direction.

'I'll need the weekend to have a wee think,' she told him.

'Grand,' he said. 'I'm in no hurry, don't get me wrong, Jane.' She liked the way he pronounced her name, slowly and carefully.

By Monday she called him and said her head was clear. She repeated her thoughts aloud on the phone.

'With my husband gone and my daughter in Perth, I can't manage. If I still lived in this area it wouldn't matter, but Drogheda is where I live.'

'Well, whatever you think, Jane, I'm not rushin' you by any means, understand? No pressure at all.'

'Oh, I do, David, but it's me, I can't see any other way. This is for the best.'

They agreed to meet again, this time outside the hardware store in one of the specially built coffee cabins that had been assembled because of Covid. People could still be together but not in one another's faces. This time he brought a wad of cash. Her eye followed his hand as he withdrew the thick bulk of notes from his denims, she could smell the fetid odour of used money, the stench of things found mostly in the human and animal gut. But the notes were good, and in no time, she'd slid fifteen thousand euros into her straw shopper.

He had to arrange the rest of the money and would be in touch the following week. Could she come? She could, she assured him. He'd bring another tranche, another twenty thou as an assurance. The rest she'd have to wait for but if she could take this in good faith, he'd be grateful.

'So we're going ahead?' He asked this suddenly, still in need of reassurance.

'We are,' she said quietly.

He wasn't tall. His hair was raven black and he wore his creased jeans well, even with wellies. He was clean too, smelling of fresh sweat. She liked a man who washed and sweated and then washed again. She wondered in a slightly guilty way what Maggie would think of all this wheeling and dealing. Or her father, who'd always hoped she'd move back to build on the opposite hill from the home house.

People came and went through the hardware centre. It was a wet day. Around them as they sipped their coffee quickly, puddles filled and a curling wet mist wandered the air. A woman she knew greeted her.

'Sure, I haven't seen you since your Mammy passed,' she said, smiling.

'Ah, no worries,' Jane answered, anxious that there would be no misunderstanding about why she was speaking to a stranger in such an intimate setting. 'She slipped away in the end, helped by the morphine nurse, I admit.'

'Ah, is that so, into the arms of Morpheus, as they say,' the other woman mused. Jane waited for her to leave.

Kelly and Jane watched as the woman hurried to her car, umbrella open.

'There's one wee thing though,' he said. 'I'd like to have the land cleared before the end of next month. I need to get moving on clearing it all, trimming them hedges.'

He explained that he didn't want any animosity with the tenant farmer who had used the fields for eighteen years. But it would have to be cleared. There were cattle and sheep and did she realise that Ivor Wilson had been subletting to Seymour Baldwin? She stared at him blankly. He nodded to reinforce his point.

'There's a wee path along the top of the high field, you know it, a wee worn path? Fenced off on both sides?' She nodded. 'That's where Baldwin ran his sheep across to get into the lake field. That's been going on this long time. Oh I'm surprised neither you nor the Mammy knew.'

He let that sit with her for a few moments. It irked her rightly, partly because Kelly thought he had one over on her, though she didn't react much beyond remarking that Wilson hadn't even sympathised with her when her mother died. As in, he hadn't driven the two miles across the road to call to the house in person. Instead, he'd sent a floppy thin card with the words *Deepest sympathies, Ivor Wilson*. She hadn't thought much of that when she read it.

They agreed that their solicitors would be writing to one another. There would be deed maps to scrutinise but all would be well. She knew it would. Then she tantalised him with an extra two acres that belonged officially to the tranche of land he was after but situated on the opposite side of the road thanks to road realignment five years before. He could have that too, she assured him. She watched his eyes brighten. He wasn't getting it for nothing. It would cost a further twenty thousand. A fair price, he'd see that, with no middle men or prats-in-offices looking for fees and percentages.

*

She returned to the town five days later and drove out to Wilson's place. He was always a name and little else. He used to deliver the annual rent promptly each November through her mother's front door in a thin envelope with no note attached. His signature on the cheque was his word. As far as she was concerned, Wilson was fairly invisible, a tenant farmer.

It was a high and twisty road, with lusty fields on either side that belonged to her. Wilson hadn't taken any particular care with the boundaries or hedges. There'd been no trimming or shaping, but he fertilised the fields and the grass was rich and green. She'd never noticed where exactly he lived, never having had to call on him before.

She found herself before a square stone-fronted house with granite quoins and a deep lead-slated roof. Around the door, a rambling rose she recognised as *Albertine* was coming into bloom. Could this be Wilson's home? She'd had no idea he lived in such a place. The glass on the windows was leaded, and the deep porch led to teak double doors. There was a shining brass knocker with a lion's head, just like the less polished knocker on their own door in the old house across the hill. Below it sat a round brass doorknob with a floral motif. Thought and money had gone into the construction of the place, which was modern.

She knocked lightly. The sound echoed within, and she could tell that the hallway was large. The door opened.

The young woman who greeted her with a vague expression had to be the daughter of the house. Married, she noted from the gold ring and large diamond on her left hand.

'Is this Ivan Wilson's house?'

The girl held a mobile phone in one hand, waved it casually at Jane and said she'd call Daddy. She was pleasant but not remotely interested in her, that much was clear. Wrapped up in her own day, not unreasonably. A teacher, Jane suspected, possibly a primary teacher in the Model School, judging by the time in the afternoon, and therefore free to be home by four o'clock. Everything tickety-boo about her appearance too. The short skirt, slim legs in snug brown suede ankle boots, a tight-fitting green top with a frill on each shoulder, and hair that flowed out and round her shoulders in an auburn mass.

No sooner had the daughter phoned her father, than Ivan Wilson appeared as if out of nowhere. She assumed he must have been down in one of the barns with the fancy metal flashing towards the back of the property and heard her car approach. He had the face of a traditional farmer. A solid face. An honest face. An I'm-no-fool flat clock face. But equally, she could imagine him in a farmer's smock, the kind of attire worn in the wilds of Sussex in the nineteenth century. At this, she suppressed a smile.

'Yes?' He faced her and waited.

'You probably know who I am,' she replied, reaching to shake his hand. His quick clasp was firm and dry, neither weak nor overbearing.

'I do indeed,' he answered politely. He waited. That made her slightly nervous. There was no follow-up, no pleasant cotton-wool kind of sentence like the kind that she was accustomed to. No *oh, you're JD's daughter, a true gentleman if ever there was one,* no *ah, wasn't I sorry your dear mammy passed, though quickly from what I hear.* None of that. So she turned square to him.

'It's about the land,' she began. 'I'll be selling.' She sounded more abrupt than she'd intended. He held her gaze in calm blue eyes which gave nothing away. It seemed this was neither good nor bad news to him.

'You have a buyer,' he stated carefully. It was not an enquiry. She nodded.

'You may know of him. He bought the adjacent fields last year. David Kelly?'

Wilson nodded. 'I know of him,' he replied quietly, shutting his lips as if afraid of letting too many words escape.

'And—' this was where she felt awkward, 'I'm afraid he'll be looking to have the land cleared of all beasts.'

'You're selling soon then?' he asked, as if something else had struck him.

'As soon as possible.'

He gathered his words like a prospector, dragging them up from some deep mine. 'It'll take me a while to get things sorted, some of the cows are in calf, and the sheep—'

'Ah yes, the sheep,' she moved quickly. 'I am aware that you've been subletting to Seymour Baldwin these past years.' Let that sit, she thought. It was her land. Time to assert herself. His eyebrows rose slightly. She hoped she'd caught him unawares. He needn't think she was anybody's fool.

Infuriatingly, he gave a slight shrug. 'Your father knew about this; I told him twenty-five years ago that Seymour would be using a few o' them fields. Your father knew.'

'But my mother didn't,' Jane countered, caught off guard. 'I don't believe you ever informed her. And if she didn't know, neither could I have known. I knew nothing of this arrangement until two days ago.'

'It was no secret. Who told you? Kelly, I suppose,' he remarked with another flicker of his brow. 'This'll be hard on Seymour,' he murmured then. 'He's an old man. Needs that land to graze his sheep.'

It was her turn to shrug. 'Well that's not really my concern, I'm afraid.' She heard herself, she sounded like a heartless bitch. She didn't like to think of Seymour Baldwin being stuck for grazing. There really was such a thing as a poor farmer, she knew, when old age arrived and the grants dried up. It struck her that she could still ask Kelly to hold off. Maybe he was pushing the whole deal through too quickly. Maybe he was too quick and she too. On the make like the greedy shit she suspected he might be, from across the border in Northern Ireland, scooping up as many acres as he could to build his little empire. Oh, they were all hopeless, these men, none of them happy, all of them grasping. Herself perhaps no better.

'I don't like selling the land, she went on, trying to adjust her tone, 'But the fact is I can't look after it. I don't live here. I'm over in Drogheda.'

'I know that,' Wilson practically whispered. 'Drogheda by the Boyne,' he went on as if deep in thought.

'By the green grassy slopes of the Boyne, indeed.' The lyric slipped out before she could stop herself or the deep blush that rose to her face. That sectarian song she'd heard frequently in the past. The Battle of the Boyne, 1690, root of so much hatred when William defeated James. A right bloodbath, the fields steeped in blood and skin and human ordure so that the place was fertilised for the coming centuries, some said, and filled with walking ghosts.

'Sorry,' she remarked. 'That song . . . I always liked that air, you know? It means nothing, just a pretty air with a sweet lyric, don't you think?' Stop digging, Jane, stop now, *stop*, you twat of a woman.

Now he was staring hard at her, his blue eyes boring into her, face like a slate of incomprehension. She'd insulted him. It was unintentional, but there was insult in those words, called up so easily, like a bunker of shit from the past ready to explode over the present in the most meddlesome of ways.

'Either way,' she tried to recover ground, 'if you could ask Seymour to please remove his sheep whenever he can. Say, within two months?'

Wilson didn't reply. He nodded assent, then turned away from her, and she turned away from him, walking briskly to her car. She didn't feel brisk though. She didn't feel much except confusion and annoyance. At herself mostly, for not understanding the ways of people who worked the land. Her late father would not have been happy at how she'd handled things.

She glanced in the car mirror as she pulled out the drive, and noticed Wilson's daughter in the porch now, watering a granite trough full of flaming begonias. Her hair fell casually forward from her shoulders as she bent down, water spraying lightly on the spring plantings. Again, that remoteness. Her world was secure. Her father owned land and had rented theirs, but all was well and they had prospered. If she sold to Kelly, she'd be landless herself. She'd have nothing but the money. She needed to think. Keep

Kelly at a distance. She could always return the money he'd slipped her.

For months afterwards, every time she sat blow-drying her own hair, an image of Wilson's married daughter's big head of auburn hair would float up in her mind. She couldn't for the life of her understand why.

17

PEACE, LOVE & PUSHPANNA

I expect mansions with lush lawns, strawberries and tennis courts but this is Wimbledon local housing. David and I drag our suitcases along Pilford Road beneath summer-swayed trees, then onto the terrace of Blomfield Gardens. Number 29 has pebble-dashed walls and a door of chipped yellow paint with loud music pumping out the open windows.

In the tiny hall, David's Aunt Alice and Uncle Kevin hug me. Kevin does a pretend squaring up to lanky David with his fists, a soft punch on the shoulder. Alice admires my hair, then pulls me into the house to meet the family. I shake hands with Bobby, Alice's eighteen-year-old son from her first marriage. He's carrying a massive stereo radio which belts out the Bee Gees current hit 'How Deep is Your Love'.

'Turn it down love,' Alice yells, 'can't hear our blinking ears with that racket.'

'Here's Katherine,' Alice goes on. 'Back from Nepal of all places. She's the adventurous one, Katmandu isn't it,' she asks. Katherine smiles and shakes my hand too. I like the look of her; long mauve muslin skirt, dark hair escaping from beneath a bandeau, a frank expression in her grey eyes. She smells of patchouli oil.

Three small boys, triplets, clatter down the stairs. 'Hello Irish cousins,' one of them pipes up as he inspects us. I'm shy of David's London relatives, their curling accents with missing h's, their casual city confidence. A tan and white rough-haired terrier races in circles around Uncle Kevin, then from room to room, barking its head off in excitement. I stroke its head and it stops, sits and gazes up at me.

'Oooh, an animal lover, you won't get 'im away from you if you give 'im that kind of attention,' Uncle Kevin says, 'sticks like glue he does.'

'He's a nice dog,' I reply. They all laugh at this, but kindly.

'So what you done in London?' Bobby enquires.

I tell him that we watched an experimental film at the Institute of Contemporary Art.

'Where's that then,' he asks.

Just off Trafalgar Square, the Mall.

'Ooh very nice,' Bobby says.

I don't tell him that it was a film in which two female bodies writhed around one another in a tangle of white sheets, or how serious the audience seemed. The day before, a silent horror film in Notting Hill which David had wanted to see. *Nosferatu*. It wasn't my idea of horror, but David said it had antisemitic undertones, so that was important. I can't wait to see *Grease* in two days' time, I tell Bobby, just to lighten things. 'A *fillim*,' he grins, teasing me for my accent.

Dinner is a free for all of chunky chips and vinegar in paper in the centre of the table and buckets of fried chicken from the local place. Everyone stretches and paws to get some onto their own plates, then pass the salt cellar around. Every so often David glances at me, checking. I smile to reassure him.

At the table, we all compete to be heard over the blare of Bobby's stereo and the big television in the sitting-room. David tells Uncle Kevin he's thinking of accepting an offer to teach history for a year at New York University, while beside me Alice is shouting about the good cut-price places in Wimbledon.

I wish they'd listen properly to David's news instead of yakking on about special discounts. Friday Specials. Uncle Kevin finished a late shift yesterday at the Waitrose depot. Before that he was a builder but after his first heart attack he gave it up for part-time work. They have the right lifting and carrying equipment in the depot, he says. There were no supermarkets in County Clare when he was growing up, people stuck to one job for life. Anyway, help yourselves to Swiss Roll, our favourite, the lemon. The triplets shoot their bony little hands out first and Alice cuts a slice each. 'Don't be greedy you lot,' she admonishes gently.

That night, David and I arrange ourselves back-to-back in the small wobbling bed in the box room. I try to let go of thoughts, to blot out street sounds, the final door-slam in the house as midnight approaches and the toilet cistern on the other side of the thin walls goes quiet. I think of my parents' silent country house, its ticking clocks in the night, fox cries outside, battering winds. In the end though, I sleep deeply.

The following morning Katherine has made fresh coffee. 'I love my coffee,' she says softly, the aroma making my stomach rumble. Already the house vibrates with the thump of Bobby's stereo, one of the triplets watches a pop programme on television and the other two jump up and down on the leatherette sofa.

'So what d'you fancy doing,' Katherine enquires, her eyelashes fluttering as she sips from a mug on which the words *I ♥ Krishna* are printed. It's the first time I've seen the heart sign and I think this is pretty cool.

David, a post-grad historian, tells Katherine we'll maybe view the Elgin Marbles. 'Of course, Maria also wants to shop on Oxford Street,' he smirks. I look at him sharply. He'd rather stay around Bloomsbury, feeling heavy and historic after seeing the Marbles.

'I don't mind what we do,' I say to Katherine, 'what do you think we should do?'

Uncle Kevin butts in then and says we should go to see King Henry VIII's palace at Richmond. 'I'll show you,' he adds. I hesitate. I get enough history from David's doctoral thesis on the Reformation. He wasn't happy when I booked Quentin Crisp at the Duke of York Theatre two months ago. I really am looking forward to that. I'd paid for the tickets with money from a landscape art competition I'd won, but David grumbled that it would have paid for some new kitchen cupboards in the cottage.

Katherine puts down her mug of coffee. 'I know,' she says, 'you could go to the new Hare Krishna centre.'

'Oh Katherine,' Alice protests, 'what d'you want to bring them there for?'

I've seen the bare-headed Hare Krishnas in Dublin, flapping around in saffron-coloured garments. Before I met David, I'd entertained the idea of joining them, but wondered how equal the Hares are and if a woman can ever become a guru.

'The new centre is opening today,' Katherine says, 'with a free vegetarian meal for everyone who joins in the ceremony.'

Neither of us has eaten much vegetarian food, but I like the idea that animals are children of Krishna too, born with a soul. At home my parents slaughter beasts every year, carving up several for the freezer and selling the rest at the market. Briefly I recall the squealing pig, and the hot metallic blood which my mother uses to make black pudding.

Within an hour David, Katherine and I take the tube to Croydon. Soon, I notice a trail of young people my own age on the street. I wonder if some are heading for the Hare Krishna centre too, and glance back at a pair of tall punks with black eye makeup and mohawks, one blue, the other green. I'd spotted them on the train. They stride close behind in black boots and studded leather waistcoats, then overtake us, chains draping from the loops in their jeans.

I enter the centre through a tree-shaded anteroom with red and black floor tiles. A trail of smoke rises from brass incense burners in several windows. The two punks clatter ahead and are welcomed by a group of followers of Krishna, who welcome us too with joined palms. Katherine smiles and bows back at them. She points to a corner of the porch where we're to deposit our shoes.

'Yes, please leave your footwear here,' a young man confirms.

The punks confer in deep voices, uncertain about relinquishing their boots to the general heap, but eventually unlace to reveal sockless feet. There's an accretion of grey filth around the toenails of Green Mohawk but the other one's feet are clean. I'm okay with letting go my platform sandals which hurt my feet anyway. Shaking his head dubiously, David slips off his desert boots, then we both look to the Hare Krishnas who appear to be in charge.

One of them points to a room off to the left, already packed with young people. From another room to the right of the porch, a waft of food reaches my nostrils. I inhale a tracery of cumin, fenugreek, ginger and coriander; lungs filling with what to me is truly exotic. I may yet convert, whatever about David, whose arms are folded tightly across his chest. Despite a low-level whiff of feet throughout the ceremony, this feeling grows.

The two punks stand opposite in the throng around the group of Hare Krishnas, one of whom steps forward to speak. I catch Blue Mohawk's eye, then look away quickly. Then the monk speaks.

'Lord Krishna,' he says, 'tells us that true knowledge and pure love may be attained only by a human being, that we must submerge ourselves into the love of Lord Krishna, through compassion.'

Away from home, it sounds simple. Away from being broke, away from parents who pity the pair of us as we try to renovate the rundown cottage at the foot of a Connemara mountain, away from David's parents who don't understand why I in particular insist on living together and not getting married. Over here, nobody cares. The Hares don't frown on anything so long as we're compassionate. I resolve to try to live with David in harmonious honesty and am keen to discuss how we might spark our lives up on returning home. Or at least whenever he finishes the doctorate and has his head out of the books long enough to spend some time with me.

The chanting begins. This is the Maha-Mantra from the Upanishad, Katherine whispers to me and David. I nod and start to chant self-consciously. The two punks are chanting an octave lower than everyone else in a grumbling way, staring hard at the floor. Gradually, I relax into it. The sound feels joyful. *Hare Krishna, Hare Krishna, Krishna Krishna, Hare Hare, Hare Rama, Hare Rama, Rama Rama, Hare Hare . . .*

The chanting ceases after twenty minutes of repetition but that's how mantras work, and despite my impatience I feel cleansed, the way I used to when Mass ended and I'd drive home with my parents. My mother would hurry into the house to check the oven temperature and the fragrant fat-encased lump of roast beef within, then set to preparing a Yorkshire pudding batter while my father walked the fields, checking the cattle.

I recall seeing a Hare Krishna centre in Dublin, along South Circular Road. I could go there even if David doesn't. It dawns on me that we're not joined at the hip and must each realise soul destiny independent of the other. Not that David believes in the soul as he's an atheist as well as a Marxist.

The Hares then invite the crowd towards the room on the right, where food is spread. I pause on the threshold as my eye absorbs the colourful dishes, like edible jewels on a huge yellow-clothed table. As I inhale the fragrances, I also watch the robe-clad young men and women who proffer this meal with such reverence, who ask nothing in return but my presence. I imagine myself in one such robe, and how graceful I could look with my long, smooth throat, my thick mane of hair. I feel a nudge in my back, quite a sharp one too, as Blue Mohawk attempts to move me forward into the room, his head twitching like a bird of prey as he eyes the laden table. Hey, I mutter crankily, but he only winks at me and grins in a sour way, so I move on.

Now everybody is grabbing and stretching, there are bowls, spoons, sauces, piled heaps of nuts, raisins and roasted chickpeas. Everything is labelled with a smiling cartoon Krishna and the name of each dish. I help myself to a creamy chickpea cauliflower dish, onion bhajis, and some pushpanna. The pushpanna is colourful as flowers, its fragrance garlanding your senses. The punks have loaded mounds of everything into their bowls, potato-stuffed samosas, sundried tomato pasta bake, pushpanna and bhajis, and indiscriminately shovel the food into their mouths. Blue Mohawk sees me looking, gives a nod of recognition and another wink. I can't help but notice his food-moistened full bottom lip and the trace of a smile like a faint heat that nonetheless reaches me.

I glance at David, who pulls at a flatbread on the other side of the table, dipping it in mango chutney before then forking up a small mouthful of black beans and creamed spinach. He's chatting to Katherine and they reminisce on the summer she spent in Ireland as a ten-year-old while Uncle Kevin's divorce was ongoing.

I return to the table after a few minutes and help myself to more pushpanna, just at the same time Blue Mohawk does. 'So what's crackin'?' he asks, offering me the spoon first. David, chewing sombrely, is now observing from the other side of the table. I shrug and move back to the wall to concentrate on my meal, and Blue Mohawk follows. We stand together in silence, spooning our food.

'Peace, love and pushpanna, eh,' he says then, looking at me with curiosity.

At first I don't respond, my mouth a cave of flavour that drifts into places still learning to be filled, cumin and coriander telling new stories to my awakening body. A black-haired woman seated cross-legged has begun to play a sitar. As my shoulders twitch instinctively into the rhythm, I pray to Krishna that David will accept a year's teaching and travel to New York without me. Now, I'd like to flow in a saffron robe through the throng and around the room. 'Yeah, peace, love and pushpanna,' I reply in a droll way, winking back at Blue Mohawk.

At this, he straightens up, I see him swallow before speaking. 'So where you from then,' he asks.

I take my time before answering, but when I do, I'm smiling.

Ackowledgements

Grateful acknowledgements are due to the following journals, magazines and media outlets which published some of these stories or versions of them: The Manchester Review, The Fiddlehead Review (Canada), RTE Radio 1, Stand Magazine (UK), Southword, The Fish International Short Story Competition, The Davy Byrne International Short Story Competition, The Incubator (N. Ireland), Take Six Anthology (Daedalus UK), Stories for the Voice (ed Neil Donnelly), Prole (UK), Studi Irlandesi (Italy), The Irish Times, The Lonely Crowd (Wales).